This is a work of fiction. All characters and events in this book, other than those clearly in the public domain, are fictitious and any resemblance to real persons, living or dead, is purely coincidental.

As a supernatural adventure story, *The Imprisonment of Lost Souls* deals with elements that might not be suitable for some readers. These include: Drug Addiction / Alcohol Abuse; Hate Speech or Slurs; Stalking and Harassment; Self-Harm, Suicide or suicidal thoughts; Graphic and explicit violence + Death on page (including death of a parent); Child Abuse; Psychological triggers such as Anxiety and Depression; and Gore / Disturbing images (in a school-based setting). Any readers who are sensitive to these types of theme / imagery should bear this in mind.

*To my friends and family*

# Chapter 1

I was heading home from school riding on my bike accompanied by my best friend Samantha Putterfield, who I met in primary school. Since then, we've been in the same classes, the same schools and conveniently enough, we live next to each other. I peered to look over at her and she seemed to have the same struggles as I did. Both of us had heavy backpacks filled with the assignments our teacher had given us. The more I thought about it, the more tired I became thinking about how hard it was going to be. My thoughts left me instantly as I saw a large decrepit wall coming into view a few feet away from the shared pedestrian and cycle path. It stood so eerily at the edge of the forest that if you were to climb over it, you would immediately be surrounded by trees. If you looked closer there was path that led up to a large abandoned building. That abandoned eerily creepy building was a school that had been shut down in 1990, according to our history teacher, but we didn't know much more about it. People in Richfield try to ignore or forget the horrendous event when those students were murdered. To this day, this ingenious serial killer remained undiscovered and under the radar. People in town believed the building was haunted by spirits or ghosts that kept it stuck in the past. Samantha and I believed the stories surrounding the school. However, many were sceptical.

I took a quick peek at the windows of the abandoned school as we drove by. For days on end whenever we bike past there going to school and back home, there's nothing to see, but today, for some reason, I spotted a male figure in one of the windows. I frowned and turned my head away. I turned back to look, but the figure was gone. Samantha noticed me lagging behind and called out to me. My mind wandered for a bit wondering who this male figure was and how he managed to be in the abandoned school but as Samantha called out to me, I snapped back to reality and hurried to her side.

Samantha and I rode to the end of the wall and turned into another street opposite the forest. We rode past a few houses before I climbed off my bike and walked into the front garden towards my house. Samantha followed me but she climbed off her bike a house down. I waved goodbye to her. I placed my bike against the wall of the garage. I locked my bike and quickly peered over to look at Samantha and watched her enter through the door. I could feel a smile on my face as I unlocked and opened my front door to enter the house.

As I walked in, my younger brother, Phillip, ran towards me hugging me tightly. I giggled in response hugging him back. Phillip is ten years old and we live with our father, Brian. Our mother passed away after Phillip's birth.

I walked into the living room and saw our father Brian sitting on his chair watching television. He didn't greet me, but I'm used to it. Since our mother died, our father had not been coping. He didn't talk much. He wouldn't get off his chair other than to work, eat, sleep or get some groceries. I waved at him and exclaimed, "Hi!"

No reaction. Brian continued watching the television. I sighed hopelessly as I told Phillip that I had to start working on my assignment for school. I gave him another hug before I left the living room and headed towards the stairs. As I walked up the stairs, I took off my backpack, holding the straps firmly in my hand.

As I reached the top step, I was greeted with a large hallway with a few doors. I walked up to the nearest door by the staircase and opened it, leading me into my room. There were some clothes on the floor that were from the outfit I wore yesterday. I placed my backpack on my bed and my phone on my side table. I started to grab the clothes off the floor and dumped them in the clothes basket so I could get them washed for Friday. As I was about to finish putting the last few clothing items in the basket, my phone began to ring. I quickly placed the rest of the clothing away before reaching for my phone and answering it. I began to walk towards my desk grabbing my pen from the pen holder.

"Hello?", I said.

"Hey, Jeanny! Do you want to go to the movies this evening?"

The familiar voice was none other than William Carter. He wasn't the "superstar" of the school, but he was amazing nonetheless. We had been dating for approximately four weeks now and before we even got together, we were childhood friends growing up together like I had with Samantha. I tapped the end of the pen gently on my cheek as he asked me his question. I shook my head.

"Sorry, William, I can't. We have so much homework to finish that I want to have a good head start on it, so I don't stress about it later when the deadline draws nearer. You're in the same class as me, shouldn't YOU be focusing on it too?"

"Yes, I know, but I am not in the mood to do it right now. I am not like you, energized to do homework right after school. Besides, for next week it's way too much to cope with."

I laughed because I knew how problematic it was for certain people in my class to do the assignment. "Haha! Yes indeed, but we could meet up tomorrow!" Silence stirred from the other side of the line.

"Sure! That could work! We can meet up in the coffee shop across the bakery around nine in the morning!"

"Wait, I thought we were going out to see a movie. No movie starts at nine in the morning," I said raising an eyebrow.

"Alright, you caught me. I was hoping to spend the day with you on Saturday. It would be nice to spend some quality time together where we do not have to focus on school for a change."

"I'd like that! But at least I can get my favourite Latte Macchiato before I meet up with you!"

"Hey, no fair, what about me?" William exclaimed.

"You should come early then if you want any! Anyways! I need to dash! I'll see you tomorrow in school!" I said with a big smile on my face.

"Alright! I will see you then!"

I could tell he was excited to spend time with me. In the four weeks we'd been together, I felt the intense homework we received had stopped us from spending quality time together. At least this Saturday can turn things around.

I hung up the phone and placed it back on the side table. I removed the last few clothing items from the ground and put them away in the basket. Phillip came in and tried to be helpful. He grabbed some of my school papers and placed them nicely on a pile on my desk. I patted Phillip gently on the head and gave him a few coins so he could buy himself some candy. I watched him jump in delight and rush out of the room. I smiled as I knew for a fact that even though he didn't know our mom that well, I could see so much of her in him. He has such a spontaneous personality that whenever I do my chores, he comes around to help, but I feel like he knows that he'll get some money for sweets as a reward. I chuckled at the thought as I walked towards my backpack and unzipped the main compartment. I grabbed a notebook and book from the fabric corner and placed them next to each other on my desk. I sat myself at my desk and opened the books. It was a book about the history of our little town. It contained most of the information about the town: from how it was settled down by travellers, to the details of its historical buildings. The particular subject I was focused on was the abandoned school next to the cemetery at the edge of the forest. According to the official death certificates, most of the students from the tragic accident that occurred are buried in that cemetery.

"Jeanny! Can you make dinner?!" said a male voice yelling from under the stairs. I closed my eyes in annoyance. I'd just sat down to study. I opened my eyes and stared at the amount of work waiting for me. 'Fine,' I said to myself.

"Coming!" I replied. I got up and hurried out of my room. I stormed down the staircase skipping the last few steps as I jumped into the living room. I peered over to look for Brian and, as I suspected, he sat back on his chair staring at the television. I pursed my lips a bit. I must admit that since we lost my mother, things have not gotten any better. It has actually gotten worst. I have been working as a maid around the house rather than living my life like a normal teenager, but then again, what "normal" teenager loses their mother at such a young age? I mean there are probably a few out there who do lose their mothers or fathers due to health problems or accidents but in truth, I miss my mother dearly. It was unfair that I had to carry the burden of keeping the house in superb condition all on my own whilst Brian sat there like a lump of meat. I was grateful to know Phillip was there to help me out as much as he could, but a little bit of emotional support from the only parent in this little family could have helped me know if I was doing a good job or appreciated.

I walked into the kitchen to the sink where I washed my hands and dried them with a cloth before opening the fridge to grab the necessary ingredients for make three meals. I was thinking of focusing on making something with chicken wings and rice. I placed the rice in the rice cooker with enough water and let it boil. I took the chicken wings out of the packet and marinated them with spices like salt, pepper and more before placing them on a tray ready for the preheated oven. Satisfied with the preparations of both meat and rice, I went ahead and fried some cut up mushrooms to go with the meal. I didn't even notice that Phillip was watching me from the corner of the door frame. He scared me when he walked up as I placed some butter in the pan so the mushrooms could extract the full flavour of the rice.

"Sorry!" he exclaimed, and I laughed in response.

"It's fine, Phillip. Could you set up the table with the cutlery and plates? Food will be done in about 45 mins."

I watched him scurry to the cabinets and drawers to what he needed to set the table. I smiled and finished cooking the mushrooms. I looked over to the chicken in the oven, then took it out and poked a few holes in it with my knife to help the meat cook inside. Placing the tray back, I decided to check up on my little brother and see how far he'd got with the dining table. Three plates were on the table and the cutlery was sitting on either side. I chuckled. "Phillip, you forgot the placemats!" Phillip looked at me in surprise before hurrying off to grab them. I walked back to the kitchen and grabbed a couple of glasses.

"What do you want to drink, Phillip?" I asked him.

"Just some juice please," he replied. I nodded and poured him some apple and mango juice from the refrigerator. I handed it to him. I followed him out of the kitchen as I looked over to Brian.

"What do you want to drink?" I asked him. No response. I gritted my teeth as I approached. I waited a few minutes to see if he saw me but he didn't shift his gaze or move his head to look at me.

"What about you? What would you like to drink?" I asked.

"You know what I like to drink," he barked. I rolled my eyes as I walked away. He wanted beer obviously. Without even bothering to look at me, he asked, "Is the food ready?" I stared at him with a hint of irritation bubbling in my stomach.

"About 40 minutes," I said in response, "I'm cooking chicken with some…"

"Yeah fine whatever," Brian said interrupting me. "Call me when the food's ready… and get me my beer!" I gritted my teeth and balled my hands into fists. I closed my eyes, taking a few minutes to gather my emotions. I stood up and left Brian alone to watch his silly programme. I walked up to Phillip who was sitting on the chair by the dining table.

"Hey, you okay?" I asked him. He nodded at me, "Yes! I am just hungry!"

"Food should be done very soon," I told him. I patted his head before walking into the kitchen to check the meat and rice. The rice appeared cooked. I grabbed a spoon, a mitten and some herbs. I lifted the lid of the rice cooker and placed the herbs inside before stirring the rice with the serving spoon. When I was satisfied with the result, I stood in the kitchen waiting for the meat to finish after delivering Brian's satanic drink.

Eventually, I opened the oven and placed the tray with the chicken on the counter. I grabbed the pan with the cooked mushrooms and placed them around the chicken on the tray before putting it back in the oven and setting the timer for the remaining time needed. I walked out of the kitchen to check up on my little brother. Phillip was poking at his plate with his fork. It was fascinating to watch as I didn't know what was going through his mind, but it seemed he and his fork were going on an adventure on an icy meadow made of porcelain. I smiled before I heard the timer go off, the chicken was ready.

Phillip, Brian and I sat down around the table eating dinner. The chicken wings sat in a bowl with the mushrooms; the rice was on a separate plate.

"Who was on the phone earlier today?" Phillip asked. I had taken a bite of rice and mushrooms. I quickly chewed my food and replied, "That was William. He was asking me out this evening to go watch a movie, but I have homework to do."

"So, what now?" Phillip asked. I watched him pick up a chicken wing with his fingers and took a bite.

"I'll see him on Saturday," I replied feeling a small smile creep over my face. I felt my cheeks blush.

Phillip looked at me for a moment and tilted his head. "I heard he was moving though…" A small sharp pain penetrated my heart as I heard those six words. I frowned and stared at my younger brother with disbelief.

"Phillip…"

I looked over to Brian as he called out Phillip's name. I waited to see if he wanted to say anything else, but he didn't. I only heard Phillip reply with, "What."

"He's moving?" I asked in a shocked tone.

"It's not even definite yet Jeanny… Don't get yourself worked up," Brian said to calm me down. I didn't reply immediately, no, in fact, I didn't reply at all. I was wondering why William would've kept something this important from me. Certain scenarios began to play in my mind as to why he wouldn't have told me. I pursed my lips a little in thought about William asking me out. Did he ask me out this evening for the very reason that he may be moving? I took another bite trying to make myself feel better but having heard what Phillip said about William potentially moving away from this little town… moving away from me; my heart just ached and felt like it was made of thin glass.

"On another note…" I looked over to Brian and Phillip. "Have you by any chance spotted a guy in the abandoned school?"

"A guy? What do you mean a guy?" Phillip asked lifting a spoonful of mushrooms. I spotted some of his rice fall on his plate.

"I saw a guy standing by a window on the second or third floor when I came home from school.

Phillip shook his head.

"I didn't see anyone. I'm too scared to even look at that building."

"What did this guy look like?" Brian asked. I peered in his direction but he made no attempt to meet my eyes.

"I only saw a silhouette of a man; I couldn't make out what he was wearing or his hair colour." I watched as

Brian shook his head and stood up. I noticed he hadn't finished his food as he left the dining room. Phillip looked over to me with a worried gaze.

"What's wrong with Dad?"

"I don't know…"

After we ate dinner, I took the dishes and the cutlery to the sink where I started to rinse and wash them. Phillip helped by drying them with a cloth. I watched him as he dried a plate I had passed him just moments ago. He began to sing with delight, "We are a good team la la la!" I smiled because it made me happy to know he was happy. As we finished the rest of the dishes and put away the food in the fridge, I headed back to my bedroom where I sat myself down at my desk to focus on my assignment. I dreaded the fact we needed to prepare a presentation on one of the subjects the teacher had chosen for us. From all the subjects I could've been given, mine was about the old abandoned school. I leaned back into my chair and placed both of my hands on my head. Why had I been chosen for a presentation about that haunted school? I scratched my head as I stared at the history book in front of me, open at a chapter on when the school first opened, who was running as principal at the time and how long the school was in service. I frowned.

According to the history book, the school had closed because of a serial killer that killed students. There were some theories that the serial killer was an elderly man who thought he was a teacher and just snapped. Other theories suggested that the killer was a former student who had a mental breakdown and yet more suggested it was the principal trying to prevent students graduating. I rubbed my temples just above my eyebrows and stared at the blank paper where my presentation should have been. How in the hell can someone come up with a theory that the principal wouldn't want to see their students flourish and pursue their dreams? I shook my head at the idea and began to worry about my presentation. How could I make an accurate report if there were only superstitions and theories about how and why the school closed and no facts. In the book itself, there was not much to report other than an account of what the school offered in terms of curriculum, who the teachers were and a list of all the students that disappeared and died who were registered there. I looked over at my alarm clock on the night table beside my bed. 7:55 PM. I grabbed my phone and dialled a number. It rang.

"Hello?" an elderly female voice said at the other end of the line.

"Hi, Grandma!" I said.

"Darling! Thank you so much for calling! How are you?" she asked.

"I'm fine! Listen, I called to see if you can remember any details about the abandoned school across from my street. You see…"

"Sweetheart, do I really need to?" she said. I noticed there was a tone of distress in her voice.

"Sorry, Grandma, but yes. It's for my presentation, you see," I responded. "I have to gather enough information about the incident at the school to get a good grade."

"Hmm…"

After a brief burst of silence while she collected her thoughts, she began to give me some details.

"The only thing your mother said about the incident was it was horrifying. She couldn't remember much, because she was unconscious by the time the police and ambulances arrived. However, she did say the students had tried to escape, but couldn't. There was a dark mist, probably a fire, engulfing them, suffocating them to death. The principal was never found, but every single student, whether alive or dead, was accounted for. Many speculated it was the principal's doing, but since there were no reports whether he survived the incident or died, his status is currently unknown. That's all I know about it, according to your mom when she came home distressed."

"She didn't mention anything else?" I asked her.

"Unless you can contact a student that survived the incident, I don't think I can be any more use to you," my grandmother said.

"Do you know if any of the students still live in Richfield?" I asked.

"I really doubt it," my grandmother said. "It's surprising your mother stayed after what happened, living with Brian and having you and Phillip. When it comes to the others, I wouldn't know. You might have to use the old-fashioned phonebook to see if any of the students are still around and willing to speak about it."

"Right, okay," I said.

"Jeanny."

"Yes?"

"Be careful. Not everyone you find in the phonebook will be willing to share their side of their story. It was a traumatizing time for everyone in town."

"I'll keep that in mind," I said.

"Good. Can I talk to Phillip by any chance? I want to hear my grandson's voice before he goes to bed."

"Yes, sure," I said. I got up and walked out of my bedroom. I walked up to my little brother's room and opened the door. I saw him sitting on the floor still wearing his normal clothes.

"It's Grandma," I said handing him the phone. He took it gladly with a big smile. He began to talk to Grandma like a speed train telling her stories about things that happened in school.

I left him to continue his conversation while I went downstairs to find the old telephone book. I found it on the small telephone table. As I grabbed it, Brian came up to me and frowned at me. "Why do you need the telephone book?"

"Just something for my homework," I said. I watched him shrug and continue to the kitchen. He didn't seem to care if I did my homework or not. I hurried back upstairs and discovered Phillip had placed my phone on my desk. I went to check up on him after placing the telephone book next to it. I wandered to his room and saw he was bashing two cars together.

"Why haven't you changed yet?" I asked him.

He looked up at me and smiled a little nervously and said, "I was waiting for you to come to tuck me in for the night and maybe read me a story to help me fall asleep."

I smiled and shook my head, "I'm not going to tell you a story because you're not ready for bed," I replied in a mock-strict tone of voice.

"Wait! I do want to hear a story!" Phillip said determinedly. He got up with his two cars in his hands and placed them in his toy basket. "I will get ready for bed, just give me like five mins."

"Okay, five minutes it is, Phillip, but don't forget to brush your teeth. I don't want to smell mushrooms on your breath," I said teasingly.

"Hey! My breath doesn't smell like mushrooms!" Phillip said protesting as he took off his normal clothes. I turned around to give him some privacy and replied, "Oh yes they do. I can smell them from here!" I smiled as I heard Phillip stomp his foot on the floor, knowing I'd managed to get through to him with the teasing. It just took him a minute to get dressed before he dashed out to the bathroom to brush his teeth. I turned around and walked into his room. It was quite a simple room with a bed, a desk and a dresser where he kept all his clothes. Just near the window, there was a toybox that our mother got for him to store all his toys in. I turned to look at the desk, there was a shelf with a few thin books resting on it mounted on the wall. I walked up to the shelf and started to browse the books. I wasn't impressed with the selection. Ninety per cent of the books that rested on the shelf were stories I had already read to him. I thought for a minute and turned around as I saw Phillip walk in with a large grin.

"I brushed my teeth, ha!" he said exclaiming with excitement as if he had just conquered a mission.

I chuckled. "Come here then and let me smell it," I said gesturing him to come closer. He skipped towards me and blew into my face as I kneeled down to his level. The minty air brushed against my cheeks as I nodded.

"Good, now get into bed. I'll tuck you in."

Phillip tilted his head and stared at me, "What about the story?"

I shook my head. "I can't tonight, Phillip…"

"Why not?" he asked me. I could sense the pout upon his face was about to lead to a temper tantrum.

I grasped his shoulders and stared at him gently. "Nothing on your shelf is interesting enough to read to you. You know the stories, they've been read to you perhaps a billion times. Tell you what, if you go to bed tonight without a story, I'll read you two new ones tomorrow, does that sound fair?" I looked at him hopefully.

I could see he was contemplating the proposal and seemed eager for a story tonight, but he nodded. "I would be okay with that if you promise you WILL read me two new stories tomorrow."

I nodded. "Pinkie swear I promise." I lifted my right pinkie in front of me to show I was seriously keeping the promise. He embraced my pinkie with his, nodding with a gentle smile. I got up and helped him climb into his bed. I pulled the blankets over him and tucked him in, so he was just a little caterpillar in its little cocoon. I sat down on the edge of the bed and softly stroked his hair as I watched him close his eyes.

"Have a good night, Phillip," I said softly. "I wish you sweet dreams."

"You too…" he whispered. I smiled as I watched him drift to sleep. I continued stroking his hair till I was fully convinced he had drifted into sleep. I gently climbed off his bed, leaned over and kissed his forehead. As I did so, I heard him mumble, "I love you, Mommy…" A sharp pain shot through my heart as he said that. I quietly and quickly exited his room closing the door behind him as quietly as possible. I didn't notice Brian had walked up the stairs and stood behind me.

"Is he asleep?" he asked. I jumped out of my as I turned around and nodded.

"Good."

I watched him walk towards the door leading to his bedroom. He opened the door and entered. I shook my head and followed him into the room. I closed the door behind me, shocked by the state of the bedroom.

"Why are you here?" he asked in a grumpy tone of voice. He stood by the bed placing a beer on the nightstand.

I shook my head profusely. "I'm here because you've not been giving me or Phillip any attention... You didn't even say goodnight to him."

"Do you want me to say goodnight to him now?" Brian said glaring from the corner of his eyes. I looked to a corner in the room filled with empty beer cans, pizza boxes and dirty laundry.

"I'm not saying to say goodnight to him now. He's just managed to fall asleep without listening to a story, but you must start to get a grip on yourself... The way you're living right now, closing yourself off from Phillip... from me..." I said with a firm voice trying so hard to get through to him.

"Look... As you said at your mother's funeral, we all grieve in our own little ways. Why don't you leave me alone, do what you are told to do and let me grieve my way?" Brian said trying to dodge the conversation.

I shook my head. "No. You're not the only one who lost someone dear. Yes, Phillip and I lost our mother and you lost your wife, but you are NOT the only one suffering from grief." I stared at him feeling tears develop in my eyes. "I've tried to stay strong since she left. I try to keep this family together by keeping the house clean, making sure we have clean clothes on our backs and keeping us fed."

"But you're not the one earning the money here, are you?" Brian said in a dangerous tone of voice. He turned around to face me and I could see a dark shadow lingering over him.

"No... I do not work. I go to school," I admitted.

"Indeed, which makes you and Phillip my responsibility and you still have to do what you are told," Brian continued. "Now if you have nothing else useful to say to me, get out."

"Yeah, whatever. Love you too..." I said snapping. I turned around, marched out of the door and slammed the door shut. I immediately walked into my room, closing my door behind me. I waited for a minute and expected Brian to storm into my room to have a serious discussion about me snapping at him, but nothing. All was silent and still. I shook my head with tears running down my cheeks. I missed my mother. The whole world was different without her. I looked at the clock for a moment, 8:45 PM. I sighed and realized I hadn't done much on my homework other than reading some theories without any facts to back them up. I walked to my desk, sat down and started to write a report of the information I'd discovered so far.

## Chapter 2

I was rolling side to side as I slowly began to wake up. I turned to look at the time on my alarm clock. It was 3:35 in the morning and I sighed, pulling the pillow over my face. I'd another bad dream that forced me awake. I grunted loudly before throwing the pillow off. I pulled back the blanket and exited my bedroom. I went downstairs and into the kitchen. I was grabbing a pint glass from the cabinet when a flashback hit me.

I sat beside Brian on a bench in a hospital. He was cradling my little brother in a blanket. I frowned as I looked at the clock. The doctor walked out of a room and approached us. Brian stood up to talk to the doctor with Phillip fast asleep in his arms. The doctor shook his head and Brian lowered his gaze before pointing at Phillip and the door.

"I'm sorry, but there's nothing more we can do for her," the doctor explained. He patted Brian's shoulder before leaving. I saw Brian sigh and walk up to me. He reached his hand towards me, gesturing me to take it. I tilted my head and asked, "Where is Mommy...?"

"She is sleeping in the meadow…" Brian said softly. I hesitated to grab his hand. I stared back at the door where my mom was.

"Is she going to wake up and come back to us?" I looked Brian who stayed, quiet, avoiding direct eye contact. I lowered my gaze. I think I began to understand that my mother wasn't coming back. I took Brian's hand, hopped off the bench and we walked together with Phillip out of the hospital.

I gasped as the flashback ended. The pint glass fell out of my hand and scattered across the tiled kitchen floor. I held my head with my hand and leaned against the counter. A tear slithered down my right cheek as I took a moment to regain my composure. I took a moment to breathe before walking to a small storage closet beside the refrigerator and the freezer. I opened the door and grabbed a dustpan and brush. I walked back to where I had dropped the glass and started to sweep it up. I shook my head in frustration for being reckless. Ever since my mother passed away, every night at 3:35, I get a vision: sometimes of the past, sometimes of the future. I looked at the shards of glass in the dustpan and sighed. I remembered when I told Brian about these occurrences during the first weeks after the funeral. He stared at me with such disgust that he immediately took me to a psychologist to have me tested. I could never forget those cold eyes staring down at me like I had gone through some sort of metamorphosis.

I stood up and walked to the garbage bin where I stepped on the pedal to open the lid and toss the glass in. I went to the cupboard and grabbed myself another pint glass. I put away the dustpan and brush before pouring myself some water from the tap. I exited the kitchen and entered the living room. I walked up to a bookshelf that hung over a dresser with my mother's picture on it. I sighed looking at the picture. She was young and beautiful with such a soft gentle smile. I softly caressed the glass where her cheek was with my finger. "I miss you, Mom." I said softly. Before her picture was a five tealight holder. I began to throw the old ones out and replace them with some lavender scented ones. I lit them with the lighter. I ran my fingers over the spines of the books, looking at their titles, before pulling one out and settling down to read it on the couch.

The book I was holding used to be my mother's. She was a talented writer and used to write loads of stories, mostly fantasy. One day, however, she decided to put all the stories together and bind them into books. Unfortunately, she never had the time to send them to a publisher. So instead, she read them to me before I went to sleep. Perhaps I should send them to a publisher and become a talented writer like my mom.

I continued reading her book, it told the story of a female elven warrior protecting a valuable object. The story was so intriguing that it kept me awake for a couple of hours before I drifted to sleep.

I awoke a few hours later with Phillip sitting next to me leaning over. I jumped out of my skin with a yelp of surprise and, in doing so, managed to scare my little brother. I panted as I looked at him.

"What are you trying to do, Phillip…?" I asked.

"I'm sorry!" he said laughing.

I shook my head and smiled. "Phillip, what are you doing up so late?"

"Late? It's early!" Phillip exclaimed. I widened my eyes and looked over to the clock over the television. It read 7:15 in the morning.

"Oh my! I need to make breakfast then!" I exclaimed grabbing Mother's book and placing it back on the shelf. Phillip watched me and tilted his head, "What are you doing?"

"I've been reading Mother's work…" I said in response. "If you want, I'll read you one of her stories this evening before bedtime." Phillip nodded and jumped off the couch. I got up, stretched myself and walked towards the kitchen. I grabbed three bowls from a cupboard and placed them on the counter. I grabbed three spoons and placed them in the bowls. Phillip came in and grabbed the placemats before leaving the kitchen again. I filled the kettle with water and pressed the button to turn it on. I exited the kitchen with the bowls and spoons, I placed them on the placemats and turned back to the kitchen to grab the boxes of cereal and jug of milk. Phillip walked in with a pout on his face. I directed my attention to him and tilted my head, "What's wrong?" I asked him.

His lowered his gaze and replied, "I was really hoping for eggs and bacon today…"

I chuckled. "I know you were, but I have to go and see William and Samantha. We're going to work on our presentations as soon as I've dropped you off at school for your trip." The smile I wore on my face disappeared as Brian walked into the kitchen. He stared at me with a disgusted look on his face. I frowned.

"Make me some eggs, bacon, toast and coffee…" he said before walking out, leaving me and Phillip speechless. I scoffed before walking to the coffee machine on the counter. I started to make Brian some coffee. Phillip watched me before he asked, "Why do you let him talk to you like that…?"

I was pouring some water in the container when I replied, "What do you mean?" Phillip looked at the kitchen door with concern. He walked up to me, so he was only a few feet away. "You know what I mean… He's ordering you around like Snowflake…"

I opened the cupboard, grabbed a large tin can and opened the lid. I began to scoop some ground coffee into the filter as I responded, "What do you mean 'ordering me like Snowflake'?" I closed the lid of the can and looked at him directly. I could tell he was very uncomfortable to speak up about what he was thinking.

"You know the story you told me, where Snowflake was a very smart husky who felt miserable because his master demanded so much from him?" I nodded and sighed because I knew the story all too well. "Well, that's how I feel you are being treated by dad. You work so hard and you haven't got any time for yourself…" I shrugged as I turned on the coffee machine and grabbed myself two pans for the eggs and bacon.

"Could you pass me the eggs and bacon from the refrigerator and a slice of bread from the breadbox please?" I asked Phillip. I heard him walk to the refrigerator and grab the ingredients I needed. He passed them to me, and I put some oil in the pans and heated up with the stove. I broke the eggs and let them cook in the hot oil once it was up to temperature. I separated the bacon and laid the slices in the second pan as I turned around to face Phillip while the food cooked.

"Look, I know it's hard to see me hard at work here around the house and focusing on school, but everything is alright…" I tried to reassure him, for what he had said was the truth. I did feel like Snowflake, hauling things for Brian and keeping the house clean. Phillip looked at me, his eyes filled with worry, and I knew he hadn't taken my words to heart. I closed my eyes and grabbed three plates from the cupboard. I placed them next to each other on the counter, then focused back on the food, putting some herbs on the eggs before fishing them out of the pan. I placed them on the plate, and turned the bacon around to ensure the other side was cooked. I went to the coffee machine and poured a cup for Brian. I handed the cup to Phillip, "Can you take this to Brian?" Phillip nodded, grasped the handle and walked out of the kitchen. I concentrated back on the pan with the bacon, taking it out and laying it on the plate. I turned the stove off and, placed the pans in the sink before taking the plates of food to the dining table. Phillip had gone ahead to put the bowls and spoons back in the kitchen and grab the other cutlery instead. I joined Brian and Phillip at the dining table.

"Thanks," Brian said without looking up from his newspaper. I only nodded in response without uttering a word. I watched Phillip poking his fork into his one piece of bacon. He placed it in his mouth and looked at me with a smile. I chuckled. "You must be so hungry…" Phillip nodded.

"I've got school soon," he said, chewing.

"Please don't talk with your mouth full, Phillip…" I said. I watched Brian drink his coffee like some sort of soda before he got up, kissed Phillip on his forehead and patted my head.

"I am off," Brian said. He walked to the living room to grab his things. I got up from the table and followed him. I watched Brian put on his shoes, grab his bag, his keys and his jacket. He opened the garage and got into his car. I watched him reverse out through the small garage door. He peered over to look at me directly before he drove off.

"Phillip! Get ready!" I said.

"But you haven't finished your food yet..." Phillip said from behind me. I nodded and joined him at the table.

"If you have finished your food, why don't you get yourself ready for school..." I said to Phillip. Phillip nodded and got up from the table.

"Okay, sis." I saw him run upstairs to grab his things. I quickly finished my food before grabbing all the dishes and placing them on the counter beside the sink in the kitchen. I knew I would have to clean them when I got home later. I followed Phillip's example; I exited the kitchen, went up the stairs and into my room to fetch my backpack, placing notebooks and books inside. I met up with Phillip by the front door once the both of us were ready to leave the house. I opened the front door and let Phillip walk out first before following him and locking the door. I grasped my little brother's hand and began to walk down the street.

We passed Samantha's house where I saw her peer through the window, waving at me and Phillip. I waved back at her, returning the salutations. Phillip's school was just down the road from our house which was convenient. There was no hassle in finding public transport to travel to school.

I entered the school grounds with Phillip. There weren't many children on the playground but there were a few. Phillip looked around as if he was searching for something or someone.

"Are you looking for something there, Phillip?" I asked him with curiosity.

"I am just looking for my friend and my teacher," Phillip replied. "They're the only ones that make school bearable…" I chuckled and saw a teacher walk out of the building. The bell rang as it struck 8:30. Phillip turned around and hugged me tightly. I embraced him firmly in return before letting him go. I watched as he ran towards the teacher with the other kids. I raised my hand in a small wave before turning around and leaving.

# Chapter 3

I walked down the street where I lived with my mind occupied. I was thinking about William and what Phillip had said regarding the possibility he could be moving. I felt saddened and somewhat depressed. I'm certain it had something to do with his parents and not with what William and I had together.

I decided to go back home to get the rest of my stuff before meeting up with Samantha. I reached my house moments later. Walking up the path leading up to the door, I looked for the key in my pocket before pulling it out. I looked at the bundle of rings and keyrings. There was a small red heart attached to it with mine and William's initials on. I smiled as I remembered him giving it to me not long ago. I inserted the key in the lock and turned it when suddenly a hand grabbed my shoulder and pushed me through the door. I began to yell in panic as I entered the house.

"Calm yourself, will you?" a familiar voice said. I immediately recognized the voice. It was none other than William himself. I turned to look at him directly, "What the hell are you doing here?! We were supposed to meet each other at nine by the cafeteria!" I observed William for a moment and his facial expression concerned me. He closed the door behind us. I thought he would've opened his mouth to try and explain his sudden odd behaviour, but he stepped forward and embraced me in a hug. I was stunned and unable to mutter a word as we stood there in silence.

"I just need to know if you're okay. I need to tell you something, but can we speak in the living room? Is anyone else here?"

I led him to the next room. "No. I dropped Phillip off and Brian's gone to work," I said. I watched him carefully as he let out a soft sigh. He offered me a seat on the couch and I took it. He sat next to me without uttering a word. I shook my head and blurted out my question, "Tell me what's going on!" I watched William sigh taking my hand in his. His hands were soft, gentle and comfortingly warm.

"Jeanny, I don't have much time..." I hesitantly pulled my hand away and shook my head.

"Just spit it out already. I can't stand this tension." William looked at me directly and nodded.

"Look... I want to tell you that I'm moving to Australia. My parents want to move there, and I'm not allowed to stay behind. Firstly, they want me to get a private

36

education and start my career young. Secondly, my mother is afraid something is going to happen. She is frightened about that old school that was shut down…"

I frowned a bit as I remembered Phillip mentioning earlier that William was contemplating moving away. I had hoped it was a simple ruse.

"Why is she frightened about it? It's closed, abandoned and no longer in use," I exclaimed.

William shrugged. "I don't know. She used to go there. I guess her memories of it are just unbearable?" I shrugged too and thought to myself that it could be a very good reason to leave this town.

"Thirdly, my dad got a new job in Australia so we kind of have to move. He wouldn't want to travel back and forth once a month just to see us, so moving arrangements have been made. I just wanted to drop by and tell you the news in person rather than over the telephone."

"Is that the reason you asked me out to a movie last night?" I asked. William nodded lowering his gaze.

"I thought I'd be able to spend it with you before I had to pack up for the trip but unfortunately our arrangements for today will have to be cancelled… I am working hard on finishing homework before leaving and I won't even have to present it. I'll hand in the paperwork and that will be it."

"William… You are lucky for not having to do a presentation, but all of this is happening way too fast! What is going to happen to us?" I asked concerned.

William shook his head. "If there was a way to make it up to you, I would, but being in a long-distance relationship… I don't think it's going to work, Jeanny. I'd rather preserve our friendship…"

I lowered my gaze. "So, we can't spend time together like going to the cafeteria or watching a movie at the cinema because you'll be gone, and I screwed up my one chance to spend time with you because of homework. God, I am so stupid!" I balled my hands into fists feeling angry at myself.

William gently grasped my hands in his. "Hey, hey, hey… You didn't know and I'm sorry I didn't explain it to you last night. I should have. In all honesty, I thought I had more time to spend with you over the next few days in and out of school but, unfortunately, my dad's work insisted we take the next flight available today."

"You're breaking up with me... You don't want to at least try being in a long-distance relationship?" I asked, looking at William with hope in my eyes. I prayed he would at least say yes to try but he shook his head. My heart felt like it had sunk in a puddle of quicksand.

"I didn't want it to come across like that, but yes... I guess we are breaking up but in a platonic kind of way. I want us to preserve the friendship we have, Jeanny... I don't want to lose it and I love you for who you are... but I don't want to make you suffer or linger for affection... I just think it's for the best for us to go our separate ways, but as friends..."

"This might be inappropriate to ask..." I asked as I tried to change the subject.

"What is it?" William asked.

"Would it be too much to ask for your mother to write me email about her experiences at the old school? It's for my own assignment."

"I'll ask her," William said. I nodded and softly muttered a "thank you". An awkward silence brewed between us. "I suppose you're right..." I said hesitantly. He looked at me. "Holding onto each other in a relationship that may not work and might lead to more heartbreak, it's best we go our separate ways." I stood up crossing my arms in front of my chest as I pulled my hands away from his. I felt my chest tightening while needles pricked at my heart.

"Look, I'm sorry it's come to this, Jeanny..." I watched him stand up. I approached and kissed him on the cheek before grasping his hand and leading him to the front door. I pulled the door open and gestured for William to leave.

"Jeanny, please say something to me..." William said. I lowered my gaze and avoided direct contact. I had nothing to say. None of the words I wanted to say to him would've been beneficial for either of us. I wanted to scream at him that it was unfair for his parents to control his career and education. I wanted to slam my fists on his chest to say that I dearly loved him like no other guy in school. I wanted to let him know that I refused to find someone else, but no words came. It was like the air had built a wall to prevent any sounds escaping my lips. William pulled out a folded piece of paper from his pocket. He grabbed my hand gently and placed the paper in it.

"My address and contact information... I must go..." He leaned in and kissed my cheek before he turned and walked off the property. I stood there trying hard to suppress the tears in my eyes. I turned around, walked in and slammed the door. I could feel the vibration of the impact tremble in the floors and walls of the house. I placed my back against the door and tears streamed like a waterfall down my cheeks. I crumpled the piece of paper in my hand.

I wiped my eyes with the sleeves of my cardigan and threw William's contact information on the small side table where Mother's picture was.

I walked to the garage to fetch my bike. I stormed off the property and hopped on my bike. As I was about to pedal away, I heard a voice behind me, "Jeanny! Where are you going?" I turned my head around and saw Samantha leaning out of her window.

"What do you mean?" I asked tilting my head a little. Samantha gave me a death glare.

"You know what I mean. William only just left a few minutes ago and now you're heading off too. What are you two planning? We were supposed to be studying together!" I sighed, frustrated, as I tried to find words to answer her.

"Go suck a lemon, Samantha!" I said turning away.

"What!?" Samantha screeched out. I ignored her and rode down the street. I heard her call out for me, but I didn't bother to stop or turn my head to look. I rode out of my street, crossed the main street and reached the decrepit wall. I frowned and rode down the path trying to ignore the eeriness coming from the building. It was soothing to know that the wall was there to secure some sort of barrier between the old school and me. I tried my hardest to avoid looking at it, but something was pulling me to turn my head and peer over. For a blinking moment, I spotted a young man around the age of 18, standing in the window on the second floor staring back at me. I shook my head before looking over again. He was no longer there. I frowned and focused back on keeping control on my bike. I was determined to go to my favourite secluded place where I could take my time and process everything that had happened in the last 24 hours.

However, something told me to check up on William before I went to my favourite spot. He didn't live that far away from Samantha and I. However, my heart raced as I approached his street slowly. I stopped my bike and stood there dead silent as I saw a moving vehicle parked near William's house with movers going in and out of the house with large moving boxes. My heart had sunk down to the tips of my toes. It was like I was incapable of moving even if I desired to. The urge to run to him was heart-wrenching enough. I wanted to hug him tightly disregarding the disapproving gazes of his family just to convince him to stay even if he had to live under the same roof as me. I knew, however, that Brian wouldn't allow it. I sighed deeply as box after box went into the moving truck. William's father was carrying suitcases from the house to what I thought might've been a rental car, because I couldn't see their original car anywhere. They must've sold it. I watched from a distance as my heart pounded painfully against my chest. I placed my hand over my chest to somehow soothe it but it was hard, especially when I saw him walking out of the house with a suitcase in one hand, a small box in the other and a backpack on his back. I held back tears as my heart leaped with joy and sorrow at seeing him. He looked miserable. He was perhaps not so happy about the move. I wondered if he was thinking of me. He placed the box in the car as he talked to his dad who was organizing the car. I guess they were taking some of their belongings with them on the plane. I watched as William climbed into the car and closed the door. I lowered my gaze, still convinced it was all just a movie flashing before my eyes. I realized that it was too painful to be here, so I said my silent farewells and rode out of his life.

I arrived at the lake that was 30 minutes away from my school and placed my locked bike against a nearby bench. I walked up to the small riverbank and sat down, staring at the ducks circling each other on the water. I placed my backpack on the sand and opened it. I pulled a notebook and pen out. I opened my notebook and began to write words on the white lined paper with my pen.

I usually come to the lake for a moment to embrace nature and meditate before going to school. The lake wasn't that large, but it didn't stop me writing notes for my own little writing project. I decided that since William had dumped me to go to a completely new country and start a new life, that was a good enough reason for me to start writing a novel. I looked over to the horizon as I went through page by page to see what I'd written so far. I read the last few paragraphs and opened a new page in my notebook. I began to write idea after idea until I was certain that I had written chapter 1. I was focused on my work but I could just hear the faint quacking of the little ducklings and their mother, the splashing in the water of fish trying to pick insects from the water's surface and small birds singing their melodies.

I was woken from my work when my mobile phone began to ring. I put my pen in the middle of my notebook and grabbed my phone from my pocket. I peered at the caller ID and it was none other than my friend Samantha. I answered it.

"Hello?"

"Jeanny?!"

"Yes?" I answered. I frowned wanting her to come straight to the point.

"Hey! Where are you?! We were supposed to be studying together!" I lifted my left hand to reveal the time on my watch, 11:45 AM. I was shocked, had I really just worked on my novel for over three hours? I quickly looked at my notebook, it revealed I was working on chapter 4. I sighed and redirected my attention to Samantha.

"I'm not coming. I have other things to worry about."

"We agreed to study together! You can't just bail out!" Samantha said from the other side of the line.

"I'm fully aware that we agreed to study together," I said to her in a scolding tone of voice, "but I can't at the moment."

"Why not?" I gritted my teeth as I hung up on her. I was getting sick and tired of her asking so many questions. I knew it was going to backfire.

I let myself fall backwards so my back hit the sand as I stared at the sky. A flock of birds flew overhead and I growled under my breath in frustration. What would she know about my issues? She didn't know William had dumped my sorry arse for a new country. I thought for a moment and cringed at the thought that William would find someone better than me. I felt tears develop in my eyes as I kept thinking of William. The tears crawled ever so slowly down my cheeks, but began to rain down like a storm drenching my face. I was crying... I was crying so uncontrollably that I got angry at myself for breaking down. A wave of depression began to clash against the walls of my subconsciousness. Random questions began to circle in my mind making me feel belittled. I began to question whether I was even worthy to be William's friend let alone his girlfriend. I started to imagine pretty girls surrounding William and my heart ached. It felt like my heart skipped a beat before a dagger pierced it making me incapable of breathing normally. I closed my eyes and shut myself away in complete darkness. The sounds of nature dimmed in my ears as I stood face to face with myself. I stared myself dead in the eyes wearing a dark demeanour with black soot-covered clothing.

"You should've known that this day would happen. The day that proves you are not wanted."

I stared at myself and shook my head. "No. William has to leave because of his parents. He wants to stay here with me but can't. Besides, he will do excellently at a new school and meet new people. Hell, he can even pursue his dreams there if he wants to."

"Are you saying this because you are telling the truth or are you trying to deceive yourself from what you are truly feeling? You're being treated unfairly and to make yourself feel better towards yourself and others, you're trying to be the better person, saying everything is alright and fine. You're not a better person. You feel no joy of seeing your beloved William go and pursue a better life without you. You want to have him all to yourself. You're a deceitful liar who is no longer desired or wanted by William or your own father."

"That's not true." I said in a strict tone of voice. "I am hurt and vulnerable, yes this is true, but I would NEVER stand in the way of William's happiness. I might be frustrated, distressed and filled with sorrow that we can't work out a compromise where we both can be happy, but I would never wish the worst for him. I know he wants me to be happy no matter what happens between us and I wish the same for him. There will always be pain and heart ache, but the friendship we hold dear to our hearts will forever conquer the burden on our shoulders." I turned my head towards the darkened abyss for a moment before placing my full attention on myself once more. "Say what you will in all your negative glory to make me feel diminished. Question me as much as you want to convince me that I am nothing or completely worthless and conquer my mind till I plead with insanity but you will never be able to subdue, is my heart and those I hold dear."

The darkened version of myself changed her facial expression in a way I never knew I was capable of. She stared at me with such hatred that the sparkle I know that I've seen in my eyes when I look at myself in the mirror, was completely incinerated by the burning fire of antagonism. I repositioned my feet and stood firm before my other self. She reached her arms towards with such a fiery desire to strangle me. I felt long sharp nails strip the thin layer of skin around my neck. I was quite aware that my other self hadn't reached me just yet, but I felt the air escape my lungs as a thick pressure began to block my airway. Something grasped my shoulders and forced me down to my knees. I winced as it felt like my skin was being ripped open slowly.

"We will see how strong you truly are when your skin is peeled off inch by inch to expose the true ugliness inside of you." Sitting kneeled down, I saw my own skin begin to peel off in front of my eyes. I screamed in horror.

I woke up from my nap as soon I saw my skin fall on the floor in front of me. I opened my eyes and looked around. I checked my watch, 13:00 PM. I sat myself up rubbing my forehead. I grabbed a few other books from my backpack as I began to read the passages inside the two books that held information about the school. I wrote down small notes in another notebook highlighting those that I deemed important to use for the presentation. I cussed under my breath. I was so invested in writing my novel that I completely forgot to start work on my presentation. Suddenly, I felt my stomach rumble and realized that I was hungry. I decided to pack up my books and stationery, stuffing them in my backpack in no particular order. I grabbed my bike, unlocking it, and decided to ride to the cafeteria where William and I were supposed to meet up.

It was about ten minutes away from the lake in a small town. It was like a little pitstop for those who had to travel to school from a long distance. I parked my bike, locking it to one of the bicycle posts, before entering the cafeteria. I decided to order a large hot chocolate with a sandwich and find a seat at the back so I could study in peace.

Placing my cup down, I put my backpack beside me on the chair and pulled out all my books. I found the pages I was on and continued to work on my presentation whilst taking small bites and sips from my food and drink. From time to time, I got up and refilled my thirst with another cup of hot chocolate, latte or a bottle of soda. When I looked up from my books, I would watch people come and go. I slightly shook my head before burying my focus back in my books.

A young barista approached me slowly and tried to get my attention. I looked up from my books at him.

"Sorry miss. It is 6:30 PM. We are closing at 7 PM."

"Oh, I'm sorry!" I said apologizing.

"That's alright," he said smiling.

"Thank you for telling me," I added. He nodded and continued to clean tables and sweep the floor. I watched him closely. He was tall and handsome. He had gentle eyes and his hair was neat. He was attractive. I stood up and shook my head. Did I really just find someone other than William attractive? I hurriedly gathered my stuff, drank the last few sips from my left-over drink, said my goodbye to the barista and left. I noticed it had become dark outside. It began to drizzle. Luckily there was enough light to unlock my bike, and I turned on the lights. I climbed onto the saddle and noticed a young woman wearing a hoodie walking into a small alley. I frowned as I felt comfortable seeing someone walking alone in a dark alley. I didn't think of much anymore as I rode away heading back home.

As I rode home, I dreaded the thought of Brian yelling at me. I didn't pick up my brother from school, nor did I prepare any food for the family. The light of my bike illuminated my way in the almost pitch-black night. A few dim lights were visible from warm comfortable homes. I began to contemplate the families in those warm cosy houses. They probably had both their parents with them cuddling on the couch watching a family movie before heading to bed. I sighed heavily once more. It was something I desired most. I wanted to hold and cuddle my mom in front of a fireplace sipping hot chocolate with whipped cream and sprinkles. I wanted to hear her voice as she read one of the stories she had written. I began to miss my mother more. I gritted my teeth and grunted with frustration. It felt like my entire world was collapsing before my eyes.

I continued cycling near the road as I peered over to the tall wall that came into my sights. I made sure that I accelerated a little as I passed the gate that led into the abandoned school. I saw a figure standing by the window on the second floor. I frowned. Did someone manage to break into the building? I slowed down and stopped at the gate. I saw a figure staring at me. I felt a shiver down my spine as if someone had shoved an ice cube along it. I shook my head, closing my eyes. As I opened them, the figure by the window had disappeared. I stopped at the gate and peered to see if there were any movements inside, but nothing stirred. I began to feel like I was hallucinating. I smacked myself across my left cheek to wake up as I saw a similar figure just standing at the other side of the rusted gate. It was staring at me with soulless eyes. He wore a white and dark blue school uniform and had blonde hair. To some extent, I was glad that the chained locked gate was separating us. I backed away and carried on with my journey back home. I felt uncomfortable and deep down I wanted to freak out. I wanted to scream but not a sound came from my mouth. How in the hell did that figure manage to climb down so quickly? Many questions occupied my mind as I biked home. It so consumed me that I barely paid attention to my surroundings. As I approached the street I lived in, a car came around the corner. We would have collided had I not swerve onto the sidewalk at the last second. I panted out of shock whilst the driver rolled down his window and started hurling some vulgarities at me. I watched as he drove away in a hurry, then stepped off my bike and walked back home.

# Chapter 4

I walked up the path towards the front door with my bike, before leaning it against the wall of the garage. I hurriedly went to the front door and as I stuck my key into the keyhole the door swung open. Brian stood in the doorway with my little brother Phillip. I looked at them both silently. I waited for either of them to scream or protest about my behaviour or why I hadn't not been in school but looking at Phillip, he was clearly holding back. Brian, perchance, had told him to keep quiet until spoken to.

"Hello…" I started.

"Inside…" Brian said with a deep disappointed tone of voice. I did what I was told and entered the house with no other words from any one of us. I took off my backpack and started to take off my jacket and shoes. After I did so, Brian beckoned to me from another room leaving Phillip in the living room. The little room was just a small storage area near the staircase with a few cleaning supplies and some tools. I entered and Brian closed the door behind me. He didn't look directly at me.

"I am very disappointed in you…" he began. "You didn't pick up your little brother. You refused to pick up your phone. You didn't study with Samantha. It's 7:30 PM and you haven't cooked food for your little brother and me. I had to actually go and get a takeout because you weren't home!" I stayed quiet as Brian began to raise his voice more, throwing all the points he could possibly find, at me. As far as I was concerned, he would've blamed my mother's death on me if he had the chance but he didn't. I did, however, think it would be better for him to blame me for existing at this point.

I was so occupied contemplating all the points he threw at me that I didn't pay attention to the questions he asked. My gaze, I realized, had shifted from looking at him directly to wandering towards the door.

"Hey! I am talking to you!" he screamed as he slammed his hand on the door waking me up from my thoughts.

I lowered my head and muttered, "I'm sorry. I didn't fulfil any of my responsibilities today when I should have. I will take it upon myself to adjust my behaviour for the better. All I ask is that you forgive me my reckless actions." Brian glared at me as I did not make any eye contact. I wanted to receive my punishment rather than continue this one-sided argument.

"Hmpf… You are grounded for a month. You are to return home right after school, no detours, no nothing. No going to Samantha's house to spend quality time or do homework. She will have to come here to study with you. I will let you have your phone, but no watching television or movies. Food is expected to be served no later than 7 PM. Am I clear?" Brian said firmly. I nodded without uttering another word.

"Good. Samantha is up in your room and don't expect dinner from me. Make yourself a sandwich if you want. Also tell your brother those two stories you promised." I nodded and waited for Brian to open the door so I could go, grab some food and meet up with Samantha. Brian eventually opened the door of his own accord. He walked out in a hurry. I suspected he was missing a game or a movie of some sort. I wasn't bothered about watching television or movies, so that rule of being grounded, didn't truly apply to me. I exited the room and walked to the kitchen to make myself something to eat. As I entered the kitchen, I turned my head and saw Phillip staring at me. He was leaning over the backrest. I could tell by the look on his face that he was angry and sad. He didn't mutter a word but turned around and climbed down to sit on the couch properly. I redirected my gaze back to the kitchen. I looked at the mess from the take out on the counter and the dishes in the sink. A sigh escaped my lips and I began to clean up. I envied them a bit. They had burgers and fries. I shook my head and made myself a ham and cheese sandwich. I wasn't fussed enough to grab something from the freezer and cook it in the oven. I took my food out of the kitchen on a plate. I walked to the hallway to grab my backpack. I proceeded up the stairs finding the door to my room wide open. Just around the corner, I managed to spot Samantha opening my drawers looking through my things that shouldn't be discovered by other people. I felt my privacy had been violated by my own best friend. Luckily, she had her back turned towards the door so I could observe her every move.

I watched her open each drawer, shoving her hands through my clothes, paper, notebooks, pens, pencils and other little trinkets. She grabbed a handful of my old jewellery and investigated it. I frowned, was she about to steal broken jewellery? She placed the jewellery back in the drawer and picked up a locked diary. She grasped the small lock and jerked it around. I suspected she hoped that the lock would give out but it didn't. She placed the diary back and grabbed a small black wallet. She opened the zipper revealing the small coin collection I had been putting together. Samantha grabbed a few of the coins and placed them in her pocket. I pursed my lips and stepped into my room as quietly as I could. I had seen enough. I grasped the handle of the door and slammed it shut as hard as I could. I saw Samantha panic, and throw my wallet into the drawer, closing it. The sound of coins clattered in the compartment. She turned to face the door and saw me standing there. She looked at me with the utmost guilt-filled Cheshire cat grin exclaiming, "Oh, Jeanny! I didn't know you'd come home! I was just eh… Lo… Looking for a pen and some paper to use to draw! Your dad said it was okay for me sit in your room to wait for you… I was wondering when you'd decide to come home." I raised an eyebrow. I placed my backpack on my bed and sat down. I peered over towards my desk and saw my penholder as clear as day with various of pens and pencils available to grasp for anyone to borrow if they needed too. Just beside it was a plastic document holder full of blank paper. I looked back to stare directly at Samantha. I wanted to stare at her disgustingly for the attempted lie, but I remained calm.

"It looks like more than just waiting in my room patiently…" I said. I saw a single bead of sweat appear on

Samantha's forehead, "I don't appreciate you snooping around in my room…"

"Like I said, I was looking for…"

"Don't test me Samantha, you're insulting my intelligence right now," I warned her. She, in return, stared at me quietly with a dumb look on her face.

"Get out." Her expression was enough to push me over the edge of patience. I was not in the mood to deal with Samantha.

"What?" Samantha asked astounded.

"I said, get out." I closed my eyes for a moment and took a minute to rub the temples above my eyes with my fingers.

"But… you said that you would tell me the reason why you didn't come to study with me!" she said. "You can't kick me out without…" My eyes flashed open. I stood up staring at her coldly. "You literally stole coins from my collection and stuffed them in your pocket, tried to break into my diary and were contemplating taking my old broken jewellery! Do you really think I'm obligated to explain anything to you?!"

"I didn't…" Samantha said.

I shook my head and interrupted her. "Spare me your bullshit. Give my coins back. I saw you steal them while I was in the room and you didn't have the decency to close the zipper of my wallet that you carelessly dropped in my drawer," I said calmly with an eerie tone, but deep down my blood was boiling.

"Fine!" Samantha said snapping. She marched up to me, threw the coins from her pocket at me before storming out of the door, and stomping her way down the stairs.

"Thanks for that you inconsiderate bitch!" I screamed after her. I sighed, walked up to my door and slammed it shut. I knelt down and started to pick up my coins. Once all my coins were collected and placed on the bed, I placed myself down next to them sighing. The door slowly opened and I didn't flinch at the sound but responded, "I swear! Get out!" I turned my head in the direction of the door and saw Phillip standing there with tears in his eyes. He let go of the handle and ran to his room. I heard the door to his room slam shut. I sighed defeated and stared at my food. I wanted to focus on my homework or write my book to get my mind distracted from all the emotions I was feeling.

I lost my appetite and stood up. I walked out of my room and approached my little brother's room opening the door slowly. I saw Phillip laying on the bed weeping softly with his back facing me.

"Phillip?" I said softly. Phillip was quiet. He continued to cry but did not utter a word. I sighed as I placed myself on the edge of his bed. I waited a minute before I spoke. I sort of expected that he would turn around and tell me to leave or hit my shoulder telling me how bad of a sister I was.

"Phillip… I just want to say that I am sorry for yelling at you and for not keeping my promise." I saw Phillip didn't budge from his current position, but he stopped crying. I reckon he was trying to listen to my words over his sniffling. I thought for a moment before I continued, "William broke up with me because, like you said, he's moving to a new country. He showed up this morning right after I took you to school." I paused, thinking of the words I needed to use to tell Phillip how I felt.

"I can't describe the emotions I'm feeling right now, for they are scrabbled together, but I feel angry and sad." A tear slithered down my cheek as I opened my heart to him. "All this anger I am feeling is because of the betrayal today.

First William and then Samantha forcing me to open up to her even though she was snooping and stealing things from my room. I'm angry at myself for yelling at you and not keeping my promise to read you two new stories." I watched as Phillip turned his head to look at me. I knew I was staring at him with a saddened gaze as he sat up slowly and placed his hand on mine. That gentle gesture made my heart jump causing me to cry more intensely than the one escaping tear.

"I am sorry Phillip," I said, "I'm just so broken right now and I don't know what to do." From me covering and wiping my eyes, he sat himself on his knees and pulled me into an embrace.

"I didn't mean to yell, or scream at you… I didn't mean to make you cry…" I said chokingly as I continued crying. Phillip did not utter a word but held me in his smaller arms as I embraced him in return. We stayed in the hug until I finally stopped crying. I realized that this emotional moment was the first one I'd shared with Phillip since our mother died. I watched my little brother take his arms from me before climbing out of his bed. He quickly left his room for the hallway. I only thought he'd gone to the bathroom to dry himself off, but I was wrong. He came waddling in holding a box of tissues for me. I, gratefully accepted and plucked a few tissues from the opening of the box. I wiped my tears and blew my nose. I watched as I saw Phillip go to his dresser and grab himself new sleeping clothes. I turned away from him so he could get dressed in peace. I thought for a moment and began a story.

*"What a strange light... Where am I? What do I hear...?' I opened my eyes to see my mother for the very first time. I heard a soft sound to my right and to my left. I turned my head to look and saw only blurry figures. I turned to look at my mother who leaned in. I felt something warm and wet brushing across my face. When looking at it more thoroughly, it was pinkish red. Suddenly, she disappeared. I called out to her but the only thing that came out of my mouth was a high-pitched whimper. I closed my mouth in fear and looked around. Beside me, I heard two of the same high-pitched whimpers. I began to shiver and seek warmth. I crawled my way around inch by inch to feel something warm brush against my thigh. I turned and curled around the warm sensation which I soon made out as one of my siblings.*

*"A large figure suddenly overshadowed us. I whimpered and tried to curl up in the corner of the nest as did my siblings. Yet a warm-hearted voice spoke to us. It was in a language I did not understand."*

Phillip walked around me and climbed into the bed. He looked extremely excited as I started a story about a small kitten.

*"It felt like a decade until my mother came back. My vision had improved and I was able to see my brother and sister. She came back carrying a small grey object which was bleeding from the mid-section of its body.*

*"It's a mouse,' she explained to me and my siblings. 'It is something you will learn to hunt and eat, but for now, nurture yourself from me.' I crawled my way closer to my mother and found access to one of her teats and suckled on it. My brother and sister did the same."*

A large knocking sound pulled our attention as Brian stood in the doorway.

"Jeanny, get to bed now." I slowly stood up and looked at Phillip.

"Have a good night, little one. I'll continue telling you the story another time." I felt Phillip's gaze upon me as I departed his room. I averted my gaze from Brian. I didn't want any more conflict with him as I hurried to my room. I heard Brian speaking to Phillip from the other side of my wall, but I couldn't distinguish what they were saying. I suspected Brian was filling Phillip's head with wrong information about me. I sat on the bed and began to eat my sandwich. The cheese and ham were no longer as cold as they had been when I prepared them. I cringed a little for I preferred to eat my food right after I had made it. I sighed deeply, struggling to chew my food as I looked through the notes I'd written. I was impressed with what I'd accomplished so far but it also had notes regarding my pain that was implemented by my antagonist attacking the protagonist.

I placed my notebook on my dresser and pulled out some of my homework. I opened one of the books I borrowed from the school's library to find more information about what had happened there. I sighed heavily as I read through the pages. It explained the basics I already knew such as when it was built, when it became a government-funded school and how many students had studied and graduated from there. The one thing that struck me as interesting an article that had been reproduced in the book. It explained how many people had fallen victim to the murderer or murderers. It continued on to say that the police had taken the only printed copy of the school's yearbook which was never published. A book that was edited each year to record which students had studied there, what achievements they had made for themselves and to increase the school's reputation. I realized that the book must be still in the police archives. It was evidence, as it said in the article, that it described all the students and staff. I thought for a moment. I knew my mother had studied at the school until she was 18 and had me nine months later as she turned 19. After she had me, she went on to study in college. It was a struggle for her, concentrating on school, writing projects, working a part-time job and taking care of me and Brian.

I quickly grabbed the library book and decided to go downstairs to talk to Brian. When I went down, he was sitting on his usual lounging chair watching the game and sipping beer.

"I came down to ask if it would be alright to call the police for a school project..." I started. I saw Brian's soul leave his body as soon the word police was mentioned.

He turned to look at me and frowned. "What for?"

"A school project...?" I repeated. "They may have some information that might be useful?"

"Oh. Yeah. Whatever." Brian said shifting his gaze away. I tilted my head a little, 'What was that all about?' I thought. I shrugged it off and went back upstairs dialling the non-emergency phoneline.

It rang a few times before a woman picked up the phone.

"Yes, hello! I was wondering if I could enquire about something for a school project." There was a pause.

*'How may we help you?'*

"For my school project, I need to find and collect evidence for a presentation due in a few weeks. I was given the subject of the abandoned school by the forest. I was wondering if I would be permitted to have a look at the school's yearbook you have stored in the evidence room."

*'I will have to speak with the chief before I can give you an answer.'*

"That's fine." I said in response. The line went silent and a random song played in its place. I sat myself down on my desk chair and grabbed a piece of paper and a pen. I was nervous as I tapped the back part of the pen on the paper waiting patiently for the woman to return.

After five minutes, the woman returned saying, *'Hello?'*

"Yes, hello. I'm here," I replied.

*'I've spoken to my supervisor and chief. We're normally not permitted to give out evidence, especially since the investigation is still ongoing. However, we can allow you to have a look at the book if you're willing to come down to the police station. You'll have to fill out a form and sign a few documents when you arrive. Will that be alright?'*

"Oh definitely!" I said, "Should I come tomorrow or a different day?"

*'If you can pass by tomorrow. Any time would work,'* the woman said.

"Okay! Thank you!" The woman responded with a *'You're welcome'* before the line went dead disconnecting my line with theirs. I placed my phone on the table and leaned back into my chair sighing.

"At least that is sorted," I said out loud, relieved. I got up and walked to the bed where the rest of my notes and books were. It would've helped so much if my mother was still around. She would've probably told me what happened on that day. I knew for certain Brian didn't go to the same school as my mother, but he did hang out with her when he was in town. I frowned and tried to remember the name of

Brian's school. Had he told us where he studied at the time? The thought swept through my head as I was determined to go to the police to investigate and study the yearbook. I continued to read the book, writing down important notes until I fell asleep.

I opened my eyes and found myself standing in an unknown hallway. I looked around and saw students roaming around as if nothing was wrong. They were carrying their backpacks or stacks of books and homework in their arms as they hurried to what I suspected was their classrooms. Lockers stood aligned along the walls as they slowly began to lose their paint job. I shook my head and thought my eyes were deceiving me. I looked around me and saw glass windows on the doors leading to classrooms began to crack. Students that seemed to not have taken notice of me at all, turned to glare at me with their skin slowly melting until there was only a mess of melted skin, veins and muscles. Their clothes melted and merged with skin, blood and tissues, creating a pool of mixed goo under their now decrepit feet. Their eyes began to burst out of their eye sockets as I screamed in horror. I covered my face, hearing screams of agony all around. The ground beneath me began to crack and tremble as the light bulbs above began to burst one after another. I raised my hands to shield myself from the falling glass and debris. I yelped as a hand grasped my shoulder. I turned my head slowly, expecting a terrifying skeleton with only the residue of skin and muscle, but to my surprise, it was a young man of about 18. He had a gentle face that made my heart beat with comfort as he gestured me to follow him. I nodded in response and began to follow him closely. Something, however, grabbed my attention, stopping me in my tracks to look behind me. A tall figure in a suit stood at the end of the hallway. He stared at me with red bleeding eyes and slowly backed away before I was grasped once more by a hand pulling me backwards more quickly. I turned and saw the young man again, but I didn't hesitate to hurry after him. We came to some sort of intersection where he grasped my hand and pulled me after him.

"Where... Where are we going?" I asked as we now seemed to be running. He did not respond to me. I began to question if I was doing the right thing. For some reason, however, I understood that whatever we were running away from, it was something bad. We approached a set of double doors with a sign saying, "Exit". I was relieved that I could leave this godforsaken place. The young man released my hand. I turned to look at him. He stared at me and mouthed something. I couldn't hear the words escaping his lips, but I somehow understood. He pointed at the doors as if telling me to leave. I approached the doors and placed my hands on either one. A bright glow emitted from my hands as the doors swung open. A bright light blinded me as I saw a feminine figure standing majestically, at least, that's what I thought. When I looked closer, there was no one there. I turned around as the young man smiled at me with such a handsome smile, but instead of smiling back, I screamed in horror as a black misty cloud engulfed and pulled him into the darkness within the hallway. The double doors closed behind him. I ran towards them and pounded my hand hard on their metallic surface. I must have slammed my hand on the door so many times before I felt the light pull me away. I screamed as I wanted to help the young man as he had helped me. The light behind me engulfed me completely until I couldn't see anything. I felt I was levitating as I drifted in an ocean of nothingness.

# Chapter 5

I walked through the doors into the coffee shop I had visited the day before and ordered my favourite Latte Macchiato. I was quite surprised to see a significant amount of people in there for a Saturday morning. I decided to sit in and write some notes for my book, write the first paragraph to my essay and perhaps some questions in case there were any detectives with enough time to speak to me about the day. I quickly looked at the clock, 10:30 AM. I opened my backpack and took out my text and notebooks. I was going to visit the police station after 12. I turned the marked pages open as I continued my work. I was glad that Brian had let me go to the coffeeshop for the day to focus on my studies. I could've gone to the library and stayed in a dark quiet corner, but personally, I wanted to sit somewhere with some sort of background noise. I looked over to the other customers who were sitting with their partners, co-workers and students. I sighed deeply, feeling an aching pain in my heart. I was glad that I was able to go out despite being grounded, for I wouldn't have been able to concentrate with Phillip's friends coming over to the house to play. I begged Brian to let me go out and study somewhere else. He agreed, on the condition that I came home before 5 PM and showed my homework. I knew some people were loud in the coffee shop but that didn't bother me half as bad as hearing boys screaming in delight as they crash toy cars together. I sighed as I took a sip of my coffee and peered at to the textbook. I was so engaged in my work that I didn't notice someone familiar sit themselves down across from me. I looked up and saw it was none other than Samantha staring at me with a drink in hand. I leaned back in my chair, crossed my arms over my chest and observed her quietly. We watched each other for at least five minutes before she spoke, breaking the silence between us.

"Jeanny... Do you have a moment to talk?" I kept silent. She looked at me very uncomfortably. "I am sorry for my behaviour yesterday. It was inappropriate and I shouldn't have snooped around in your room. It was so unnecessary for me to break your trust like that."

"Mhm..." I said staring at her. I waited for her to continue.

"Can you please forgive me?" Samantha said, looking at me with eyes full of hope.

"You tried to steal my coin collection. You lied to me."

"I swear I won't ever do it again," Samantha said in a reassuring tone of voice. I, myself, wasn't all too sure whether or not to take her words as the truth.

"You know, Samantha… It's hard to believe you since you betrayed my trust," I said.

Samantha lowered her head gazing down at her drink. She nodded.

"I understand…"

"Do you?" I immediately stated. She continued avoiding eye contact.

"I feel like you're just apologizing because you want to know what happened between me and William so you can spread little lies in school and find ways to try to steal things from me."

Samantha looked up at me and I could see in her eyes that it was exactly why she came to apologize; however, I couldn't just accuse her of something without solid proof to back it up.

"I'm not convinced you truly are sorry. I feel like you don't cherish our friendship, even though we grew up together." Samantha lowered her gaze once more and I could tell instantly.

"I do cherish our friendship… but I'm dying of suspense to know what happened between you and William."

"You know… Friendship is more than just gossip and secrets," I said watching her. "You're making this more about yourself than worrying about how I'm doing. I'm heart broken, Samantha. You, in my room snooping through the stuff in my drawers, and William leaving me that morning would've left anyone in a frenzy."

I paused because I felt tears developing in my eyes. I had to restrain myself from crying in public with the stinging pain.

"I needed you to be my support, but you just shit on me with no care in the world!" I slammed my right fist on my right leg feeling the impact on my muscles. I admit, I was angry at her, at William and, most of all, I was in pain. I felt Samantha's gaze as I felt my heart break and crack within my chest. A man who was cleaning up some of the other customers' dishes walked up to my table and peered at us.

"Is everything here alright?"

I looked over at the man tempted to tell him, "No". I wanted to beg him to escort Samantha away and keep her from coming back into my life, but instead I said, "We're fine. Sorry if I was a bit loud."

The man nodded. "Alright, call me if you need assistance or help."

I nodded but I knew I was not okay. I was lying through my teeth to a stranger and he had probably sensed that I was not okay. Samantha looked at me as soon the guy had left us alone.

"Thank you," she whispered.

I glared at her. "Don't thank me just yet. I wanted him to escort you out of here, but I'm not that cruel." I said coldly.

Samantha placed her cup on the table. "Jeanny, please forgive me. I didn't know that William showed up yesterday morning. How many apologies does it take for you to forgive me?"

"It is entirely up to you…" I said. "How many times do you want to mutter those words until they are but meaningless and wasted gasps of air?" I stared at her as she began to contemplate what to say next.

"Words will always mean something," she said.

"Not if they're overly used..." I said in response. "What was it you were looking for in my room?" Samantha began to sweat and stared down at her cup.

"I..."

"If you're truly sorry and you care about recovering our friendship, you'll tell me what it was you were looking for..." I said.

"I..." Samantha said still looking down at her cup.

"Well?" I said impatiently, eagerly waiting for her response.

"Remember that gemstone necklace you showed me? I wanted it. I noticed you hadn't worn it for a couple of weeks, so I thought you might have gotten bored with it. I really just wanted to wear it before returning it to you," Samantha said. I stared at her with utter shock. I clenched my fists and gritted my teeth.

"Me... getting bored of my necklace because I haven't worn it for a few weeks...?" I said staring coldly at her. '*Oh, if stares could kill, honey,*' I said to myself.

"I am sorry, Jeanny… I just want to know where you got it so I could buy myself one…" Samantha said.

"This particular type of necklace is not something you can just buy off a hook in some kind of gemstone store…" I spat.

Samantha frowned and looked over to me. "Jeanny… Are you… okay…?"

"No… I am not okay Samantha…" I said. "That necklace you so desire, was from my mother, which she left me in her will along with a book she wrote before she passed and also, the lock to the silver necklace has broken; it's currently being fixed at a jewellery shop." I watched as Samantha's face turned completely pale.

"I… I didn't know…" Samantha said softly, obviously taken aback.

"How would you? You're completely and utterly oblivious! How did you get so stupid?" I said. I stood up and began to pack my things, but Samantha stopped me as she stood up and got out of her chair.

"You stay… I'll go. I know when I'm not wanted." She took a couple of steps towards the exit before she turned around and looked at me. "You're right… I have become close-minded and selfish. I'm sorry that I put you through so much trouble and wasn't there for you when you needed a shoulder to cry on. I'm sorry that I've become such an unreliable friend. I hope you can forgive me one day…" She lowered her gaze before she left. I watched her leave and walk down the street. I fell back into my chair and rested my head in my hands with my elbows supporting my weight. Words and emotions began to fill my mind and heart. It was hard to breathe as I began to digest what had just happened. A piece of me wanted our friendship to go back to the way it was, where we spent time together and shared our common interests with one another, but another piece of me just wanted to tear that girl apart piece by piece. I lowered my hands and let them hang either side of the chair. I placed my forehead on the table and tried so hard to keep my tears in check.

I must have sat in this position for at least a couple of minutes because the guy came back asking me if I was alright and if I wanted another drink. I sat myself straight in my chair and nodded. I explained to him that I was just frustrated with my schoolwork, that it was taking a toll on me and my classmates. He seemed to understand and brought me another hot beverage that I paid for on the spot.

I began to focus back on my work until I knew it was time for me to go to the police station.

The police station was just two doors down from the coffee shop. Police cars and vans were parked outside the building. I walked to the door that had a sign saying, *'RECEPTION'*.

I opened the door and walked into the building seeing a rather spacious waiting room and a large counter behind what I suspect was bulletproof glass. There was no one at the counter but there was a small button that would probably notify an administrator that someone was there. I walked over and pressed it gently. I heard a small, muffled ring in the back. I waited patiently and took a moment to look at the flyers around the room. There were posters focusing solely on domestic abuse. There were others focusing on trafficking. There were wanted posters and missing persons posters on their own designated wall. I was concerned at the amount of wanted people and people missing. There were other posters referring to other crimes such as theft, assault etc.

"Yes?" a woman that seemed to have appeared out of nowhere said. I jumped as I turned to look at her.

"Hello! I think you've been expecting me? I'm the student who would like to look at the yearbook?" I said.

"Ah yes," the woman said. She grabbed a folder and started to gather some documents and pass them through the little slot on the counter.

"Read through them and sign when you're ready," she said handing a pen over with the documents. I grabbed them and began to read while I stood at the counter. I didn't notice that the lady had disappeared halfway through the documents I was reading. She must've known it would take a while for me to read through each one. I signed the documents that required a signature and rang the bell once more when I knew I was ready.

The lady returned after a few minutes and took the documents as I gave them back to her through the slot. She looked through each one to ensure I had written all the information and signed them.

"Wait here for a moment. There will be someone to take you in."

"Okay," I said. I walked to one of the seats and sat myself down as I watched the lady disappear again. I was a bit intimidated by her. She had a strict face. I didn't have to wait long before a tall police man approached me from a side door. He kept the door open. "Ms. Jeanny?" he said.

I got up and approached him. "Hello." I said.

"Pass me your backpack," he said. I frowned but reluctantly handed over my backpack. I remembered that in the documents it was necessary for them to check any bags I owned for weapons. He went through my backpack and handed it back to me when he was satisfied there weren't any.

"Follow me," he said. I walked through the door before he closed it behind us. He walked past me and led me to a small dark room with a large mirror. I knew from criminal TV shows that it would be a two-way mirror glass. I saw there was a long table in the room with three chairs. One on one side and two on the other. In the middle of the table was a box that looked old and worn.

"Please. Take a seat," the police officer said. I looked at him and nodded. I approached the table and sat on the chair. The officer walked over to the other side of the table, grabbed a pair of gloves and slipped them on.

"If you could please do the same," he said handing me a pair. I nodded and did so. He waited until mine were on before he opened the box.

Silence filled the room as neither of us spoke a word. I watched him cautiously as he pulled out a sealed plastic bag with a book in it. He placed it on the table with the seal facing him. He opened it and gently took the book out placing it on the plastic bag.

I watched as he passed me the book across the table and sat down on the chair.

"There you go. Feel free to go through each page and let me know when you're finished." I nodded and reached out for my backpack, grabbing my notebook and pen to take notes. I opened the yearbook and started to study each page. The officer watched me as I studied. He wasn't staring the soul completely out of my body, but it was enough to not feel overly comfortable.

I read the profiles of all the students who attended the school at the time and looked at the officer. "Do you have the list of people who lost their lives…?"

"I can take it out for you," he said, standing up and rummaging in the box. He grabbed a folder and placed it in front of me. He opened it and gave me the list of the deceased. I thanked him and placed it in front of me, correlating it with the yearbook. I was surprised at how many reports of those who had lost their lives were unknown. It was even more concerning that the autopsy reports came back with heart attacks, strokes and other concerning conditions as the cause of death, although through the reports of each student, the medical reports itself of their overall health were one hundred percent. It was unclear to the pathologists why all these healthy students had suddenly lost their lives in such a short span of time.

I was horrified when I read through the reports. All the colour drained from my face as my mind raced like a marathon. Questions raced into my head like a rollercoaster, making me incapable of writing all of them down on paper. I could feel the gaze from the officer as I scribbled all my questions down. I continued reading through the yearbook until I stumbled upon my mother's profile. I paused as I read through it and they described her almost perfectly. I softly placed my finger over her picture and held back my tears. I didn't want to cry in public over a picture in a decades-old book. I continued my work corresponding reports to the profiles until around 3:47 PM. I panicked because I had about one hour left before I was expected home, yet the amount of work I still needed to do was immense. I looked at the officer, "Would it be possible for me to come in for another day to finish the last few pages?"

"I'll need to confirm it with my superior, but I think it would be alright. You'll have to sign more papers when you arrive."

I nodded, "Yes that's fine. I need to go home otherwise I'll get in trouble." I took off my gloves and placed them on the table.

"Trouble?" the officer said.

"I am grounded and on a strict regime of what I am and not allowed to do," I said. The man nodded understandingly as I got up and started to pack my books and notebook.

"Thank you for your time, and for letting me access the archives of this open case. It helps a lot," I said to the officer.

"You don't have to thank me. You'll have to thank the detective that allowed you to access it," The man said. He grabbed the yearbook and placed it back in the plastic bag sealing it. He took the death reports and reorganized them back in their folder. Placing the evidence back into the box, he sealed it, staring at me. I finished packing my bag and followed him out of the room. As we left, I was greeted by a middle-aged man extending his hand towards me. I hesitantly grasped it as he introduced himself as Detective Nate.

"You must be Jeanny?" I nodded.

"Do you think you have time to answer some questions?" he asked.

I shook my head. "I'm sorry, but I'm expected home before five tonight. Grounded for disobedience."

"Ah, yes," the man said smiling.

"She'll need to access the evidence again on another day," the other officer said.

"When do you plan on returning to continue your work?" the detective asked.

I shrugged. "Would tomorrow be alright? About the same time?"

"That shouldn't be much of a problem. But tomorrow, will you be open to answering some questions?" the detective asked.

"Do I need a lawyer?" I asked nervously.

The detective chuckled a little. "Unless you've committed a crime you wanted to confess to, I doubt you'll need a lawyer. It's just some routine questions, very simple ones."

"I don't mind answering any questions you have, but I do really need to go home," I said. The detective nodded and showed me the way out. The officer who had been in the room with me earlier took the box and disappeared into a back room.

I followed the detective to the reception area and we said our goodbyes. I walked out slightly satisfied with the amount of work that I'd accomplished, but disappointed by the fact I didn't manage to finish writing all my notes. I returned to my bicycle and rode back home.

I arrived at home just in time. When I stepped in through the door after locking my bike up in the garage, Brian came up to me immediately stretching his hand out and beckoning for what I presumed was the homework I'd been working on. I removed my backpack and opened the zipper. I lifted my notebook out and handed it to Brian. He opened it and began to read some of my work. I stood there in the hallway waiting for a response. I was a bit nervous, because I wasn't sure if he would think my work good enough. I remembered some of what I'd written down. I'd struggled with the first few sentences of the introduction but ended up crossing them out aggressively. I became frustrated and anxious. I feared I wasn't capable of writing a thoroughly researched essay for the assignment. I, myself, believed it was not worth talking about the dead in a presentation, but how was I supposed to pass my class this year if I refused?

"You did some work, but I expected a bit more from you…" he said about, what I assumed, was the introduction section of my essay.

"It is hard to work with limited sources…" I said. I saw his eyes widen as he closed the notebook and tossed the thing on the ground before my feet.

"Absolutely despicable!" he shouted glaring at me. "You left the house to about that ridiculous abandoned shithole?! What kind of school are you even going to?!"

"It's an assignment for literature and presentation…" I said trying to explain. "It's to prepare us for university, these kinds of assignments happen a lot during the first year…"

"Tch! University? You're not qualified to go to university if you skip school! You're not going out anymore whether your little brother has his friends over or not."

I frowned. "I can't help it that this is my assignment! I don't like working on this project and subject either, but unfortunately, if I want to pass this year's class, I have to!" I leaned down and picked up my notebook.

"That subject is just a disgrace," Brian spat.

"Why? Because it used to be Mother's school?" I replied.

I waited and stared at Brian as his face became pale. "How did…"

"The police have gathered evidence that I am permitted to go through to find clues, recorded documentations about the day and aftermath for my school project. The case itself, however, is still open even after all these years. Remember… I'm going through every detail to write an essay about the tragedy and the closing of the school. Yes, I've even researched the fact that Mother used to study there as I found her picture in the yearbook…"

Brian shook his head. "You shouldn't write this presentation… This school meant a lot to your mother… you would be disgracing her memory."

"Her memory? People have died! I think her memory of all those people she knew being torn apart and murdered would have left a blood-stained impression in her mind when she was still alive! What difference does it make now?" I watched as Brian walked up to me and slapped me across the cheek. I stared at the ground in shock as I felt his hand made contact with my skin. I turned to look at Brian as he stared at me taken aback. He took a few steps back and hurried into the living room. I had my hand on my cheek as I put my notebook in my backpack. I marched straight into the kitchen and began to prepare something to eat for myself, Brian and Phillip.

I decided to cook a simple meal of rice, vegetable and some simple meat. Phillip walked into the kitchen, but I didn't notice as I was leaning over the counter cutting vegetables after placing the rice in the rice cooker. Phillip came to stand beside me and placed his hand on my arm. I looked at him taken aback as I was not aware he had walked in.

"Are you okay?" he asked.

I shrugged and said, "Yeah, I am good."

Phillip turned to look at the entrance and focused his attention back to me. "I saw what he did. You didn't deserve that."

"I was out of line…" I said as I continued preparing food. Phillip did not buy it as he shook his head.

"No. I don't believe that… He had no right!" I looked at him from the corner of my eyes and realized that he was on the verge of tears. I placed the blade down and kneeled, so I was level with him.

"Look, Phillip… Yes, it was wrong, but he earns the money and we live in his house and he pays the bills. The only thing we can do is obey him."

"But not to the point where he's slapping you…" Phillip said. I was truly astounded by my little brother's intelligence.

"Even Ms. Birkely doesn't slap my classmates; she gives them detention." Phillip added on, "Why can't Dad give you detention?"

"He did… Sort of," I said. "I'm grounded."

"He can't double ground you though," Phillip said. "Or can he?"

"He can decide to extend the time I'm grounded for or remove it completely."

"It's not fair!" Phillip said sulking.

I shrugged. "I know." I softly patted his head before going to the sink and washing my hands before continuing to prepare the food. I asked Phillip to set the dining table with plates, cutlery and cups so I could just walk in with the pans. Brian, however, sat himself in his usual chair not uttering a word.

When the food had finished cooking, I brought the pans to the table, placing them carefully on the placemats. I began to scoop food onto both Brian's and Phillip's plates. I watched as Brian began to eat, tearing into the piece of meat with his knife. After putting a piece of food in his mouth, he glared at me. "Once you've finished scooping Phillip's food onto his plate, get me a beer from the fridge." I stood still for a minute staring at Brian with disbelief and eyes filled with hatred as I scooped the last few vegetables onto Phillip's plate.

"I can get it…" my little brother exclaimed getting on his feet.

"No," I said whispering.

"I asked your sister," Brian spat, "She can do it."

I placed a hand on Phillip's shoulder and looked at him. I smiled at him as he returned my gaze. I turned and walked back into the kitchen. I heard Brian spitting sentences to Phillip such as, "Girls like your sister need to be taught that we men are superior to them. If you give them too much rein, they'll try to buck you out of the saddle. Keep those reins tight and you'll have an obedient mare."

I opened the fridge's door and stared at the bottle of beer directly in front of me. I clutched the handle tightly as I pictured smashing the bottle across Brian's head. I grabbed the bottle and placed it on the kitchen counter. I opened the drawer and pulled out a bottle opener. I closed the fridge as I grabbed the bottle once more and walked to the dining room. I went to Brian and placed the bottle in front of him with the bottle opener.

"Here you go…" I said.

I began to walk to my seat when Brian said, "Wait!"

I turned to look at him. "Yes?"

"Grab me a pint glass."

"Can't you just drink it from the bottle?" I asked.

"I can, but I don't feel like it today. Pint glass."

"Fine," I said walking back into the kitchen and grabbing a pint glass swiftly from the cupboard. I hurried back and placed the glass on the table. As I tried to walk to my seat again, Brian opened his mouth once more.

"Could you not open the beer for me?" he said cutting into a piece of meat.

"I can, but the bottle opener's right there…" I said.

"I'm trying to cut my meat, and you haven't put any food on your plate yet. So, do it."

I sighed, frustrated as I peered over to look at Phillip. He was frowning and stared at me with such concern. I walked up to Brian, picked up the bottle opener and opened his beer. I placed them back on the table and hurried to my seat. I began to scoop my now-cold food on my plate. I avoided eye contact with Brian as I began to eat. The vegetables were starting to get soggy and the meat was getting tough to chew. I refused to stand up and put my food in the microwave. I watched as Brian finished his meal and got up. He grasped his beer and began to drink it directly from the bottle. He didn't even pour the drink in the glass! I bit hard on the piece of meat in my mouth, biting my tongue in the process as he left the dining table to watch television in the living room.

The frustration within myself was replaced by the pain I felt. I tried to soothe myself, but astonishingly, Phillip reached over and placed his small hand gently on my arm. He looked at me with a saddened gaze I hadn't seen before. He stood up and took my plate. I tried to stop him, but he shook his head.

"Please let me do this for you…" he said walking to the kitchen. I heard the microwave door open and close. Loud beeping notes played as Phillip pressed the buttons.

Moments later, I heard the microwave rumble to life faintly in the kitchen. Minutes later, Phillip arrived and placed my plate back down in front of me. Steam emitted from the vegetables and meat as I began to eat the now-newly warm food.

"Thank you…" I said softly to Phillip. He nodded in response.

"He's acting like a jerk… I don't like it," Phillip said sitting himself down and continuing to eat.

"Don't use such language…" I said warning him.

He shrugged. "Screw it, Jeanny. I don't like seeing you like this. Please let me help."

I shook my head. "You can't help, Phillip. I'm capable of taking care of you and myself, much as I appreciate your support. Next time, however, when he asks me to do something, let me just do it. This way he only gets angry with me but not you."

Phillip shook his head. "It's unfair." I nodded as I didn't disagree with him.

We both finished our food quickly before we washed the dishes together. This time Phillip wasn't singing as he dried off the dishes I was cleaning in the sink. I sighed, peering at him from the corner of my eyes. I knew in the back of my mind. I had disappointed him and yet here he was still helping me and staying close to my side. I smiled softly before returning my attention to the knife I was scrubbing.

My eyes wandered to a figure outside standing by the fence where a streetlight illuminated the street. I clearly saw he was wearing the same white and dark blue school uniform. I remembered that one night when I biked home and saw him standing on the other side of the rusty gate. How did he know I lived here? How did he find me? I frowned as I put the knife I had just cleaned in the rack to dry.

"Jeanny...?" Phillip asked as he watched me whilst drying a plate.

"Phillip...? Why don't you go upstairs and get yourself ready for bed...?" I said. I kept my eyes locked on the figure.

"But... I'm not done helping you with the dishes..." Phillip protested.

"I can manage the last few by myself. You need to get your sleep. Now go." Phillip shook his head but did what I asked. I heard the drying cloth being smacked on the counter and heard small footsteps exiting the kitchen. I continued staring outside as I watched the figure walk away until he was out of my sight. I frowned as I finished the rest of the dishes by myself. At least I knew my little brother was safe upstairs getting ready to sleep.

As I finished, I walked out of the kitchen, turned off the lights and walked up to Brian who sat watching a game on the television.

"May I ask you a question?" I said looking at Brian. He acknowledged me for a moment. He lifted a finger to signal I had to wait until whatever happened in the game finished. I sighed shaking my head.

"Have you ever seen a boy with a white and dark blue school uniform?" I asked as I saw that the game had come to a halt with the referee holding up a coloured card.

Brian glared at me and shook his head. "No. I don't know anyone like that."

"Even with blonde hair?" I asked. For a moment I saw that his face turned pale for a split second before it returned to its drunken colour.

"No! Just leave me be, girl!" he spat as he grabbed the remote and turned up the volume.

"Ugh!" I said as I turned and walked out of the living room. I went directly to the front door and made sure it was locked. A knock caught my attention from the kitchen window. It was peculiar that I could pick this up with the loud noise coming from the television. I knew it was a bad idea, but I had to investigate what the noise was.

I walked into the kitchen and looked around. There was nothing out of the ordinary from what I was able to see, it being dark and all. However, the knock became more distinct from the window near the backdoor. Installed in the backdoor was a small window covered by a small curtain. I remembered Mother wanted to have a small window so she could take a moment to watch the birds in the early morning before preparing breakfast. I smiled a little remembering a bit from my past when the third and fourth knock pulled me back to reality.

I walked up to the backdoor ensuring that the lock was in place. I knew the door had been locked this whole time, since Phillip and I don't really go to the garden to play anymore. I stared at the curtain and was nervous. I knew that in horror movies there was always someone hiding somewhere in the middle of the night. I reached out, holding the edge of the cloth, hesitating to pull the curtain aside to reveal whatever was behind it. I withdrew as I knew it would be a stupid thing to do. There was a glass window! If I wasn't careful enough and there was a burglar on the other side ready to smash the glass, I could get seriously hurt. I turned away and began to walk towards the dining room, but as I took one or two steps away from the door, there were two additional knocks. They didn't appear to be aggressive or demanding. I gritted my teeth as I rapidly approached the door and shoved the curtain aside. I had my eyes closed as I did so, but hearing no other sounds, I found the courage to open my eyes slowly. There was no one standing there to stare back at me. I sighed, a bit relieved as I began to giggle a little out of nervousness and at my own stupidity. I was being worried for no reason. I turned away and rubbed my forehead with my fingertips. A loud knock made me tremble in my knees as I turned around to face the door. I approached the door slowly, looking behind me making sure Brian or Phillip weren't there to scare me. I turned my head back to the small window when I gasped in anguish and dropped to the floor. There, I saw the face of the male figure I had seen at the gate near the abandoned school. His face and clothes were covered in fresh blood. I screamed as the nightmare began to play in my mind. Darkness consumed me soon after as I remembered my eyes closing.

There was only darkness. The monstrosity I had seen of the guy completely covered in fresh blood with a knife sticking out of his chest horrified me. It did not take long for a nightmare to completely consume me. I feared for my safety and felt alone.

# Chapter 6

I walked down the hallway of the school. I looked around and saw blood on the floor and walls. The guy I saw earlier at the window stood at the end of the hallway. He stretched his hand out and beckoned me to follow him. I hesitated and shook my head. Suddenly, the sounds of a deep growl echoed behind me. I cringed and turned my head to look behind me. Nothing. I redirected my attention back to the guy as I heard another growl, now a bit closer than before. I began to run down the hallway. Whatever it was behind me, it wasn't friendly. I ran towards the guy and saw a blinding light behind him. I continued towards him feeling a hungry negative presence overshadow me from behind. I began to panic as I quickened my pace away from this dreaded negativity that began to embrace me inch by inch. The only thing I wanted to do was run away from whatever was chasing me. Looking ahead, the boy seemed so far away. I began to run towards him as it felt like I was being chained to something heavy as if someone tried to pull me down into the depths of the ocean. I screamed as I tried my hardest to reach the boy, I ran as fast as my legs were able. I reached out to him with my hand extended as a blinding light engulfed me.

I gasped as I sat straight up in my bed. I lifted my hands to look at them as I scanned the room for familiar faces. One face was familiar to me, my grandmother sitting on a chair half asleep. I realized I was panting and sweating. I looked at my duvet and some crystals, such as white quartz, obsidian and amethyst, rested near my feet. I leaned in and placed my hand on my grandmother's.

"Grandmother?" I asked. I looked at her face. She was in her early seventies and mother to my deceased mother. She had nicely combed silver hair and her clothes were simple. A nice embroidered spring blouse with a matching long skirt. I watched as my grandmother slowly opened her eyes. She peered at me and jumped to her feet.

"Jeanny! Are you alright?! You had me worried!"

"I'm fine, Grandmother. I've just got a little headache, that's all."

My grandmother sighed heavily. "Your little brother called me to come when you fainted. Of course, me being in the city, I couldn't come straight away, but I managed to convince a taxi driver to drive me here."

"What about Brian?" I asked.

"That knucklehead brought you to your room but didn't bother to check on you," Grandmother said scoffing.

"How's Phillip?" I asked.

My grandmother smiled, "You worry about everyone except yourself. He's fine. Do you need a painkiller to battle that headache of yours?"

I shook my head. "No, I'm fine, but pray tell. How long was I out for?"

"It's 8:45 AM right now. You were out cold for hours…"

I gasped and widened my eyes. I was taken aback. "What?" I said. "Are you serious?" My grandmother nodded.

"I need to catch up with my homework…" I said slowly climbing out of bed. I noticed that I felt relatively weak and my grandmother pushed me back into bed.

"You should be resting… Your health is more important than some classes."

"Okay…" I said climbing back into bed.

"I'll be back. I'll get you some porridge." My grandmother turned and exited my room. I watched her leave as I lay down flat in my bed. I stared at the ceiling.

"I really need to catch up with my homework… I need to go the police station to finish my research and talk to this detective…" I listed the things I needed to do and slapped my hand on my forehead as frustration washed over me. I didn't notice my little brother had waltzed his way into my room.

"Jeanny?" he asked.

I removed my hand and turned my head to look in his direction. "Phillip? Are you alright?"

"No fair! I wanted to ask you that!" he said pouting. I chuckled.

"Okay, let's just pretend you asked me first," I said smiling. Phillip approached me and sat on my bed.

"Dad said that you're sick…"

"I am a bit, but I'm feeling better now," I reassured him.

"Are you sure? Dad said you needed to go and see a special doctor."

"Did he now? What type of doctor?" Phillip nodded. He opened his mouth to mutter a word when Brian walked in. My grandmother was right behind him holding a tray with a bowl of porridge, a small plate of bread and jam and a glass of juice.

"You should eat the porridge while it's still warm." my grandmother said placing the tray on my lap. I sat up quickly, so the tray was not on me while I was laying down.

"Thank you…" I said looking at my grandmother with a smile. Phillip looked at both my grandmother and Brian. I could read on his face that he could sense the intensity between them. Simply put, they despised each other with a passion. Phillip had the right idea. He climbed off my bed and tried to get out of my room as quickly as possible.

"I'm just going to my room…" It was clear he was speaking to me. He hastily left my room, leaving me behind in this deep unknown abyss of hatred.

"I need to talk to you," Brian said. My grandmother grabbed the chair she was sat on before and placed herself closer to me.

"Just eat, sweetheart," she said placing her hand on my wrist.

"I need you to leave, Marion," Brian said. "This is important, between the two of us."

"Whatever you have to tell my granddaughter; I'm pretty sure she doesn't mind me listening in."

I nodded and stared directly at Brian. "Whatever you have to say to me, you can say to Grandmother."

I could see Brian's face light up with frustration. "Fine," he muttered.

"You want to talk to me about some sort of illness? You think I'm sick, don't you?" I stared at Brian. Having my grandmother by my side made me feel so much more confident.

"Look, I don't know what Phillip said but I believe you've inherited the same cursed sickness as your mother." I felt my grandmother's rage boil within her. I knew what Brian was referring to. He didn't cope well with paranormal stuff and I knew both my mother and grandmother were what people call witches. I reached over to my grandmother and took her hand in mine. She didn't look at me directly but squeezed my hand. It was like she knew exactly what I was trying to say.

"I don't understand..." I began playing dumb. "I am 100 per cent healthy apart from collapsing into a faint state yesterday, but still."

"This has nothing to do with a physical illness but rather a mental one." Brian said.

"Wait a minute... Are you...? Do you think I am crazy?!" I felt my grandmother squeeze my hand and I calmed down a little. Brian extended his hand out to stop me uttering another word.

"Just hear me out. Your mother saw things that did not exist. She claimed to have seen people who passed away. When you asked me yesterday about seeing a guy or a silhouette of a guy, I feared for your wellbeing." I looked at Brian with disbelief. I was not convinced he cared or feared for my wellbeing.

"Just because I saw a guy by the school, it doesn't necessarily mean I'm mentally ill!"

"What about you screaming at nothing yesterday?"

"I saw a guy completely covered in blood!" I stopped myself. "I must have been tired yesterday if I started hallucinating. I haven't been sleeping enough."

"I can't take any chances. You're going to see a doctor on Monday!"

"The hell she is!" my grandmother exclaimed.

"I am her father and legal guardian! She will go to a doctor when I tell her to! If I arranged a dentist appointment for her, she would have to go! She's only 16 years old and still my responsibility!"

"You can't just do this to me! Yes, you make the arrangements for my doctor and dentist's appointment, but I'm not going to the doctor because you think I'm crazy!"

"Enough, Jeanny! You're going to the doctor and that's final!" Brian shook his head and I crossed my arms and pouted.

"You're seriously going to take her to a psychologist?" my grandmother asked sternly. It was obvious she had a lot of things to say to Brian.

"It's only for her wellbeing," Brian spat. I watched as he exited my room before staring at my bowl of porridge. Small streaks of steam emitted from my food. My grandmother placed her hand on mine with such gentleness and smiled at me warmly.

"Finish your food and when you're ready…" She pushed something in the palm of my hand. "Sneak your way out to my house…" I looked at her in disbelief and gripped the item in my hand firmly. I nodded at my grandmother.

"I'm sorry make you bike all the way to my home…" my grandmother said, "…pack your homework and a few days' worth of clothing. Make sure you're dressed warmly, okay?" I nodded as I began to eat.

"I'll distract the two downstairs so you can slip out unnoticed." I nodded once again to show I understood the instructions. I watched as my grandmother exited my room. I opened my hand to reveal a key. A key to my grandmother's house. I clutched it tightly in my hand and finished my food.

As I finished the last bite of food, I walked to my closet and opened the door. I spotted my backpack on one of the lower shelves. Phillip or my grandmother must've placed it there for safe keeping. I picked up my backpack and placed it on my bed. I checked inside to ensure that my homework was inside. Luckily, all the textbooks and notebooks were still there. I returned to the closet and snatched myself some clothing from the other shelving units. I grabbed some extra simple school supplies like pencils and pens.

I noticed the note William gave me the day we had our talk. I stared at it for a bit and thought about it. I remembered how angry I was that day but now wasn't the right time to cry or throw disapproving temper tantrums. I grabbed his contact information and shoved it at the bottom of my backpack.

"At least it wouldn't give Brian or Phillip the idea to contact William…" I said softly. Satisfied with the things I'd packed away, I grabbed my grandmother's key from the side table beside my bed and placed it in my jeans pocket. I grabbed the loop handle of my backpack and exited my bedroom.

I walked down the stairs. I had to make sure I didn't make any sound whilst descending. I peeked around the corner as soon my foot was on the first step. I spotted Brian sitting on his favourite chair whilst Phillip had grabbed his favourite toys and was playing at the dining table. I knew that it wasn't safe for me to proceed to the exit. I had to wait. I froze in place as I saw Phillip shoving his chair back and walk to the living room. I spotted my grandmother emerge from the kitchen carrying another tray of snacks and drinks. She managed to spot me and looked away immediately.

"Dad, can I watch some cartoons now?" Phillip asked.

"Sure, come on." I watched as Brian leaned over and picked Phillip up placing him on his lap. Brian grabbed the remote and changed the channel. The screaming of a talking duck came from the television. I began to sneak towards the dining room. The unfortunate thing about this house's layout was that the front door and the foyer were directly connected to the living room. The only thing that separated the two was a half partition wall. Usually, the staircase would either be right at the foyer, but mother decided to change the interior layout.

I reached the dining table and kept myself low. I began to sneak my way towards the foyer as my grandmother placed the tray on the coffee table.

"I have some apple rose tarts that I've baked today. I thought you three might want some."

"Is there any whipped cream with it?" Phillip asked.

"I can grab one from your fridge, but I don't think sugar is always good for you. That pie has already…"

"Just give him some…" Brian said interrupting.

"He'll be hyper before bedtime…" my grandmother said sternly.

"That'll be Jeanny's job to deal with," Brian said staring at the television.

"She needs rest! She can't always be expected to tuck Phillip in or do the house chores. You'll need to take up some of that responsibility, Brian!"

"My rules, Marion. If you don't like it, just leave and go back to the city with your cat," Brian spat.

"With Jeanny feeling unwell? Absolutely not!"

I gulped as I heard them argue with one another in front of Phillip. I balled my fists as I couldn't condone adults arguing in the presence of a child, it was just outright unfair.

I snuck towards the front door as quietly as possible. I quickly took my jacket from the hanger as I approached the door. I grasped the lock and turned it. I placed my hand on the door handle and opened it. Suddenly, I heard Brian call out my name. I closed my eyes before turning to look.

"Jeanny?"

Brian and I had a very quick exchange of gazes. He had gotten to his feet staring at me. "What do you think

112

you're doing?!" he exclaimed furiously. I watched as Brian tried to reach me, but he tripped falling face flat on the floor. I peered at my grandmother who I suspected had tripped him with her foot. She mouthed at me to go. I didn't hesitate after that and escaped through the door to the outside. I closed the door behind me. I figured that it would only take a few moments for Brian to catch up to me.

I ran away from the door and hurried to my bike. I inserted the key to unlock my bike. I swung my backpack across my back, grabbing both bike handles, and ran to the gate. I heard the door behind me open and rapid footsteps soon followed. I quickly hopped onto my bike and pedalled as fast as I could. Brian was closing in. I managed to get up a significant amount of speed, but Brian still chased me all the way down the street. He tried his hardest to catch up and made several attempts to grab me, reaching out with extended arms. I accelerated to create a gap between me and Brian. To my good fortune, I turned around a corner. From the corner of my eyes, I could see Brian slow down to the point he stopped in his tracks panting. I sighed, relieved as I continued on my way to my grandmother's house in the city.

# Chapter 7

I stopped at a bench near a park in the woods that they used to bring classes from schools to do scavenger hunts. I stepped off my bike sighing and took a good look around. I saw a small camping spot nearby where one could start a fire and spend the night. I knew I had to take a moment to regain my stamina. I had been biking for a while trying to avoid any obvious places where Brian might find me.

I took off my backpack and plumped it on the bench beside me as I sat down. I stretched my back along the backrest and felt my bones crack which gave me a real sense of satisfaction. I reached over towards the handle of my bike and pulled the sleeve of my jacket. It slid flawlessly into my hands. I put it on and zipped it closed. It was getting cold outside. Feeling a bit more secure, I released a long sigh. I looked up at the clouds and saw a couple of birds flying overhead.

"They seem to have no problems going wherever they want to go..." I said. After a few minutes of restoring my energy, I got up and swung my backpack on my back. I hopped onto my bike, pulled out my phone and called my grandmother. She, however, didn't pick up the phone. I left her a voicemail saying that I would be late arriving and decided to bike towards the police station. I needed to finish my assignment.

Grandmother Marion lived approximately 24 miles away. If I had a car, it would've been just a 30 to 45-minute drive. I continued cycling down the dirt road back into the village and headed straight to the police station. However, I really wanted to be in the city. I thought about Phillip and how concerned I was with him staying with Brian, alone.

I got off my bike, locked it and wandered back through the reception area. There was already another person standing at the counter speaking with an officer. I sat down on one of the seats and waited. It must've been about ten minutes when Detective Nate came from the backroom and gestured me to follow him. I frowned as I had expected to wait for the officer behind the counter to hand me the documents to sign again. Was this breaking protocol? I got up and followed the detective. He guided me into a room and extended his hand. "Your backpack please."

I willingly gave him my backpack so he could have a look inside. He had a quick browse before he permitted me to proceed inside.

"Please take a seat," he said.

My gaze followed his hand as he gestured to a seat propped against the table in the room. The box with the evidence stood alone in the dim light. I walked in and approached my seat. I pulled it back and sat on it.

"Before I give you the book…" the detective began, "may I ask you some questions? I am aware you were alright about doing so, yesterday. However, I need your consent once more, on record this time." He pulled out his digital recorder and shoved a stack of paper in front of me.

"If you can please sign these papers and confirm you consent to me interviewing you today," Detective Nate said.

I looked to him and gave a nod. "I give consent to Mr. Nate to interview me."

The young detective gave a warm-hearted smile and nodded. "If you can please sign, we'll begin the interview." I grasped the pen that sat lonely on snow-white blankets of fallen trees covered in black scribbles. I hurriedly searched for the pages which required my signature and signed them. I returned the stack of papers across the table and Detective Nate began to question me.

"What is the reason you wish to gain access to an open investigation?" he asked.

"I was hoping to research some information for my school project," I said.

"Why are you researching information on the abandoned school for your project? What kind of project is it?"

"I was assigned this project by my teacher who said it was a presentation we needed to prepare for the end of the year," I explained.

"Is your teacher in any way linked to the investigation or related to any of the victims?" Detective Nate asked.

"I'm not sure." I replied. "It's a possibility but I can't say for sure."

"Alright. I might speak with your teacher about that," he said. "Are you in any way related to any of the victims?"

I looked directly at him. "I'm the daughter of Phoebe. She went to school there. However, she survived the tragedy." I watched as he wrote the information on a small notepad nodding.

"And your father is?"

"Brian," I said with a bitter tone. The detective looked up at me from his notepad.

"Something wrong?"

I shook my head. "Just a few disagreements at home," I said quickly. "It's been hard since my mom passed away."

"My condolences," the detective said redirecting his gaze to the notepad on the desk. I waited patiently for the next question but it never came. Instead, he proceeded to finish the last notes and open the evidence box. He passed me the book and death report. I thanked him and took out my notebook and pen to start researching again.

"I hope you don't mind me being here," Detective Nate said. I shook my head and opened the yearbook to where I'd left off.

I skimmed through the yearbook creating a statistic profile on how many people died from "unknown" causes and how many survived. Fortunately, two thirds of the school managed to survive the tragedy; however, it was still a large sum of people who lost their lives.

I began to write about the teachers and the principal who were introduced at the end of the book. Time must've moved quickly by as I focused and studied, for when I checked, it was late afternoon and I still had a long trip ahead of me to reach the city. While I was writing down notes, the detective asked me some relevant and irrelevant questions about what my Mother used to study, how she survived the tragedy and how she met Brian. I noticed that the detective seemed very interested in Brian since he asked where he studied as a teenager and why he was there at the school when he should've been in school himself.

Suddenly, a face appeared in the book that made my heart skip a beat. There he was. The young man I had seen in the windows at the abandoned school and who had stood by the door scaring the living spirit out of me. The colour in my face drained as I stared at the boy. Detective Nate tilted his head a little with concern spreading over his expression and asked.

I nodded as I refocused. "Yeah… I'm fine," I said. "I thought I recognized this boy, but I'm not sure."

The detective leaned over to look at the picture. "I think he's one of the victims." He grabbed the death report and nodded. "Yes, he is."

"Ah okay." I said as I didn't want to explain that I had seen this spiritual entity haunting me. I double checked all the notes that I'd taken corresponded to the reports and the book, and was satisfied with my work. I looked at the detective and thanked him for the opportunity to finish my research. As I did so, I wrapped up my notebook and pen and put them back in my backpack. The detective returned the book to its plastic prison and placed it in the cardboard box. The death reports were placed gently on top of it. I stood up slowly and stretched. I could feel some of my bones cracking. The detective followed my lead and extended a business card to me.

"This card contains all the information you need to contact me if you have any more enquiries." I took it appreciatively and extended a hand to him.

"Thank you again for your time. If I was able to help at all by answering your questions, I'm glad I could contribute something."

The detective smiled. "You did, a little. I wish you all the best for your presentation and if I still have any questions, I'll contact you, alright?" I nodded as we shook hands and left the room. He led me outside to the reception area where I checked on the time. I cussed a little under my breath as I calculated approximately how long it was going to take to reach my grandmother's house.

I didn't dwell too long on it as I returned to my bike and hopped on. The sun begun to descend in the distance and the chilly air started to pick up slowly. I went on my way following a few dirt roads leading out of the small village and turning on the lights on my bike.

I continued along the track only to discover a busy road up ahead. I felt relieved that I no longer had to bike on off-terrain paths. In general, I didn't mind cycling in the country, but eventually all the sharp stone edges and sliding gravel would make it more difficult to control my bicycle.

I took a few bends before my front wheel finally made contact with concrete road. There was just a few more miles left for me to conquer before reaching the city's border. I was hoping to see the sign that welcomed newcomers to the city. I told myself I was going to make it. I encouraged myself with how relieved I would be when I finally reached my destination. I saw a lot of cars drive past me sticking close to the speed limit. My mind wandered to the thought of buying my own car one day. Just the mere thought made me giddy and excited. I would have the ability to drive anywhere I wanted to go. I thought of the places I wanted to visit. I thought of my mother who had a large magnetic wall installed in her library room. She had magnets from all the places she had been. It would be nice to add magnets to the collection.

I saw the city's sign come into view. I sighed relieved that something so simple made me happy.

*I wouldn't be surprised if my grandmother is already home, but she did give me her key. What if she's been waiting for me to arrive? What if Brian kicked her out and she's been stood outside her house for hours on end?* I was overshadowed with thoughts of concern. I began to cycle quicker once I entered the city's limit. I vaguely remembered where my grandmother lived: past the main street on the way to a semi-rich neighbourhood. The city wasn't that big in comparison to New York or Chicago but it was confusing enough to get lost in. I continued down the road ensuring that I was not caught up in the traffic. I knew that it took me two to three hours to get to the city all the way from home, but being away from Brian was a relief.

I continued to work my way down main street feeling the awkward stares from people who lived in the city, especially the ones that looked rich. I ignored them as I looked at the shops. There were some shops that caught my immediate attention and I made a mental note to visit them when I had the chance. I knew I didn't want to spend too much money, especially in charity stores, since I'd been saving up all the money I received for my birthday and Christmas. In addition, I knew that me and Phillip had our own bank accounts but we weren't allowed to access it until we were 18. My mother was resourceful and had split her savings for me and Phillip, but she hadn't told Brian about it in her will.

I remembered when I was called into the office. Brian insisted that he wanted to be in the room, but under strict instructions from the will and executor, he had to wait in the waiting room. The same played out for Phillip, but a couple of years later when he was a bit older, Phillip's reaction was priceless when he told me, but he was also grateful to know Mother had thought of us.

My mind wandered to a nearby playground in a large park. I smiled as I remembered going there regularly when I was at my grandmother's house every weekend. Speaking of which, I spotted my grandmother's house in the next street and I raced towards it as fast as my tired legs were able. I finally arrived at the house and stepped off the saddle of my bike. Panting, I climbed the steps to the front door. The door opened as soon I reached the top step, and a friendly face greeted me as she pulled me into a warm embrace.

"You are finally here!" my grandmother exclaimed.

I was so surprised to see her that I stuttered, "I… I thought…"

As if knowing what I was going to say, she interrupted me and released me from our embrace. "He told me to get out ten minutes after he chased you down the street. I took a taxi home and I was hoping to see you on the way, but to no avail."

I lowered my gaze. "I was trying to avoid being spotted by Brian," I said embarrassed.

"There's nothing for you to be ashamed of…" my grandmother said reassuring me. "You did the right thing avoiding main roads, but at the same time, it's reckless. If you were not near people and you were kidnapped, raped or killed, that would've been my responsibility and guilt to bear."

I shook my head. "I could take care of myself… if that happened."

"Against one or multiple people?" She stared at me intently. I looked back at her silently. I had no answer.

"I thought so..." my grandmother continued. "Anyway, come in. You must be exhausted." She turned and walked in. I followed her closely into her warm comforting home.

As I followed her in, I saw loads of different types of crystals on the side table in the foyer. There was an amethyst bonsai luck tree standing elegantly in a bowl of sand with tea candles around it. I continued into the living room.

"Just take a seat, Jeanny..." my grandmother said as she sat on her favourite chair.

"Would you like something warm or cold to drink?"

"Please, something cold," I said.

My grandmother nodded. "I'll get you some sandwiches or snacks, if you want."

"Just snacks, please," I said as I watched my grandmother.

She looked at me. "Why don't you write down what's been troubling you on a piece of paper. I'll help you after I'm done." I leaned back into the couch and felt a surge of pain down my spine. I looked over to my grandmother and nodded. I watched her leave. I groaned softly, I closed my eyes and tried to stretch my back. After my grandmother left the living room and I took a few minutes to crack my back, I stood up and walked to a table with a drawer. I opened it and grabbed a piece of blank paper. I grabbed a pen from my backpack and sat back down on the couch. I began to write.

Unaware of what I was doing, my grandmother was in the kitchen preparing drinks and snacks for the both of us. A black cat rested on the window sill. It lifted its head up as my grandmother walked in.

"She looks so much like her mother," my grandmother muttered as her cat silently watched her. She turned the kettle on and the water began to boil. She opened a cupboard and grabbed a few serving plates, a mug and a

pint glass. She closed the cupboard and opened another to grab a roll of biscuits, remove them from the packet and place them on the plate. She walked to the fridge, opened it and grabbed a bottle of ice tea that she brought back and poured in the glass. It was just enough for one. She placed the empty bottle aside for recycling as she continued to talk to the cat.

"Don't you worry. I'll tell her. She's ready." The cat flicked its tail. "I just hope she'll take it better than I expect." The cat tilted its head and stared at Marion.

I sat on the couch with my knees against my chest. I'd written a few paragraphs on my piece of paper. My grandmother walked in with the drinks and snacks tray, and placed it on the coffee table.

"Thank you." I said softly. I watched as my grandmother nodded and sat down beside me.

"You want to tell me what's going on? Have you written it down?"

"Sort of." I handed the folded paper to my grandmother. She took it with both her hands as if handling something delicate. I watched her close her eyes. Knowing my grandmother, she was having visions of me, Brian,

Phillip and possibly the young man that terrorized me. She opened her eyes and stared at me. "Do you want to add any details to the things that are bothering you?"

"I'm actually not sure if I want to share more details or not."

"I have to admit that I need to share something important with you in regards to myself, your mother and your future. It's up to you whether you're ready to face it." I stared at my grandmother with a mixture of curiosity and anxiety. I took a moment to look around the room. Pictures of my mother stood radiantly above the fireplace in frames. A bookshelf full of books stood in the corner of the room. I stared at them for a while. Some of the titles interested me and some didn't. My attention was pulled towards my grandmother's black cat wandering in with it's tail high before it jumped onto the couch. I watched as it pressed it's claws in the fabric and curled up.

"I'm not sure if I'm ready to know," I said reconnecting my eye contact with my grandmother.

"If it helps, I saw you, Brian, your little brother Phillip and that young man soaked in blood." I stared back at her in silence. "I know a few things about that young man, but it's not up to me to tell you. He has been reaching out to you, but you'll have to find out what he wants."

"What do you mean?" I asked.

"You'll have to open yourself up to a new world beyond the living," my grandmother said. "You remember Brian saying that you'd need to see a 'doctor' to check your mental state?" I nodded gently. The mere thought that Brian thought I was mentally ill, annoyed me.

"He said the same thing to your mother."

"I don't understand. He claimed I was mentally ill," I said annoyed.

"The gift you carry isn't an illness but rather a blessing, though also a curse."

"Grandmother, can you please stop talking in riddles. I don't understand."

"You have the gift to communicate with spirits that are trapped between the realms of the living and the dead." I shook my head in disbelief.

"That's not possible," I said.

"If it is not possible, how is it possible for the boy you saw, to try and reach out to you?"

I shrugged. "It could be just a reoccurring nightmare or just a boy I picture in my head to get away from all the stress and anxiety of school?" I watched as my grandmother chuckled. She didn't seem all too convinced by my theory. I frowned in confusion.

"That's exactly what your mother said when I told her, but she knew what I said was true."

"I'm not sure about this... It's impossible for me to think I could communicate with ghosts," I said. *The mere thought of talking to people who no longer exist seems far-fetched. If people were indeed born to see, let alone speak with, the dead, then no one would have the fear of death,* I thought to myself, *...but what if that young man truly was trying to get my attention?*

"I am fully aware that all the information I've been throwing at you might be overwhelming..." my grandmother began, "...but with a little bit of training here and there, you'll be able to communicate with spirits like you would in school with your friends. However, there are some instances when you are not speaking with a spirit but rather something else entirely."

"There are more than spirits out there?" I asked.

"Yes, but you do not have to worry yourself about that just yet. The real question is whether you're willing to learn the basics of your gift?" I turned to look over to my mother's picture and smiled.

"Will I be able to contact my mother?" I asked softly. My grandmother sighed as I looked for a hopeful response.

"Jeanny, our gift does give us the ability to see and talk to spirits but it will not allow us to choose whom we want to see or speak to. Your mother and I helped a lot of families around here by freeing the spirits of their loved ones from their eternal prison between the two worlds. I can't say who you will see on your journey, but it is not impossible that you might stumble upon your mother if she chooses to show herself to you."

"Has my mother contacted or shown herself to you since she passed?" I asked hopefully. My grandmother shook her head and a drop of disappointment trickled into my heart.

"You will see her eventually..." my grandmother said staring at me. I could feel she was just as disappointed as me, if not more. I lowered my gaze and felt this sickening tension between us. I wasn't able to describe it other than that it made my stomach turn.

"I was thinking of going to do some grocery shopping tomorrow morning, would you like to accompany me?"

I nodded. "Of course."

"Anyway, grab yourself a snack and your drink. After that, you can go to bed if you like. You must be exhausted with the amount of cardio you've been through today." I nodded and lifted myself off the couch to grab a few biscuits. I ate them slowly as my grandmother began to tell me all the other possibilities of my so-called gift. I listened to her with one ear due to a sudden surge of exhaustion washing over me. I quickly grabbed my drink once my biscuits had all been eaten.

Once I'd finished my drink and eaten my biscuits, I wished my grandmother a good night and headed upstairs to the guest room.

# Chapter 8

I woke up in the early morning, sat up in my bed and rubbed my eyes. I frowned as I looked around in the guest room. It took me a moment to realise I wasn't in my own bed, in my own room, and not with Brian and my little brother. It felt rather odd waking up in a room I wasn't too familiar with. The room was simple. I was sleeping in a double bed with two nightstands on either side and a small desk in the corner with a chair. At the foot of the bed was a large towel waiting for me. I knew that it was there for me to take a shower if I wished to take one. In all honesty, a shower did sound like a delight to my ears. I climbed out of bed and grabbed the towel. I opened my backpack and grabbed a change of clothes. I left the bedroom and went straight to the bathroom to take a shower.

As I came out of the shower, fully dressed and hair tied back after using a hairdryer, I joined my grandmother downstairs to eat a simple breakfast of eggs, toast and bacon. Once we had finished our cups of tea, we left the house and went a few blocks down the road. We walked into a large supermarket with a clothing section with the rest of the store devoted to regular grocery shopping. I followed my grandmother as she went aisle to aisle following her shopping list. My mind was pondering on what she had said the evening before and I noticed that the young man that had appeared to me in the abandoned school, as well as scaring me at the backdoor, hadn't appeared in my dream. I wondered if I was too far away for him to contact me.

When we arrived back home, I walked into the living room with my grandmother carrying the grocery bags in one hand and a box of candles and incense in the other. I leaned down and placed the two boxes on the coffee table. I left the living room to put things away in the kitchen. While I was in the kitchen, my grandmother removed the items from the coffee table and placed two pillows on the carpet either side of the table. She placed herself at one end, lit the candles and turned the main light off. I joined her not long after. I sat across from my grandmother. I looked at her with concern. "What is going to happen with my school?" I asked.

My grandmother smiled. "Don't worry. I said you were studying on the project you were assigned to and are too far away to get to school and back. They will send your assignments for the week to this address so you won't have to miss anything."

"Oh…" I said.

My grandmother tilted her head. "Would you rather go to school?"

I pursed my lips and shrugged. "I don't know. I can't be seen there because of Samantha and I can't risk seeing Brian."

My grandmother nodded her head, "Hence why I decided to get you out of school for at least a week, as long as you can fulfil your assignments."

"Oh definitely," I said.

"The reason I asked for you to join me is so you familiarize yourself with what your mother and I did to help trapped spirits during our séances. I will try to ask if Kaia can join us. She is someone who died mysteriously and was seeking help for her quest."

"Died mysteriously?" I asked.

"Yes, but before we proceed, do you see the box of salt on the table?" I nodded.

"I need you to form a circle by pouring salt on the carpet around us," my grandmother explained. I frowned and looked at her in the dim light.

"Why a salt circle?" I asked.

"There are various methods to keep malevolent spirits at bay but I prefer using either chalk or salt to protect me. Thanks to the carpet, I can't really use chalk to draw a circle around us, hence salt. Make sure it's not too thin a layer when you draw the circle," my grandmother said sternly.

"Okay," I reassured her, following her instructions. Once I was done, I inspected it again before entering the circle with her.

"Alright, so as you are aware, Jeanny, Kaia died mysteriously and had told me she seemingly passed from something relating to her heart. The doctors don't how a young 37-year-old woman passed away when she had a very strong heart."

"Wasn't it a heart attack?" I asked and my grandmother shook her head.

"They ruled that out. The heart did not appear to have been damaged by a heart attack. Her younger daughter found her in the kitchen when she went in to make her a drink."

"Her daughter lives without her mother now?"

My grandmother nodded. "Yes and no. She lives with her father now, like you and Phillip living with Brian. But unlike you two, she's an only child."

"Must be lonely… to be an only child."

"It has it's pros and cons," my grandmother responded. "It is up to you which one of them you'd prefer." I shrugged as I watched Marion place both of her hands on the table palm up.

"Place your hands on mine," she instructed me. I followed her instructions. She closed her eyes and began to incantate, "…Kaia, if you are here, please make yourself known by giving us a sign…" I watched my grandmother carefully. Apart from the movement of the fire, there was no other sound. I opened my mouth to mutter something to my grandmother when I heard a loud knock. A cold shiver slithered down my spine as I froze.

"Kaia, if that is you, please knock on the door again." Silence followed again. I thought for a moment it was just a coincidence that there had been a knock on the door. *It must've been the cat,* I said to myself. Moments later we heard another knock on the door.

"Can you please show yourself, Kaia?" my grandmother asked. Silence. I looked around to see if I could spot anything unusual when suddenly I gasped in shock. Behind my grandmother was the fading face of a young woman.

"S… She is..." I whispered attempting to notify my grandmother but she only nodded at me. It was as if she already knew this entity was going to appear.

"Thank you for coming, Kaia…" my grandmother said calmly. I watched as Kaia approached us standing, well floating, at the edge of the coffee table. She looked down at me before locking eyes with my grandmother.

*'Were you able to find it?'* Kaia asked.

"Yes, I was able to keep it safe." My grandmother pulled her hands back before placing a box on the table wrapped in a black cloth.

"It's in here. What do you want me to do with it?"

*'Please deliver it to my daughter but don't let anyone else open or touch the artefact.'*

"Your daughter is too young to handle this much responsibility," my grandmother commented. I sat there in silence.

*'There is no one else. It has to go to her.'*

"Alright, I will see what I can do," my grandmother responded.

*'Thank you,'* Kaia said. I watched as she nodded to my grandmother and began to vanish. My grandmother placed her hands on the table once more. I embraced them with my own as she began to incantate a few more words. After a moment, she slowly got up and blew the candles out.

"Well, that's that," my grandmother said. I got up and turned the main light on.

"Can I learn how to do that? You know, to do a séance?" I asked.

"Of course. It's easy to learn the steps but you'll need training," my grandmother said. "In the meantime, I'll have to do this for Kaia."

## One Week Later

I walked down the entrance hall of my grandmother's house as I exclaimed loudly, "Alright, I am off, grandmother!"

"Do be careful when you head back! Just because Brian knows you were with me, be prepared for him to show up and try to drag you to the doctors again." I turned around as my grandmother walked up to me.

"If he does, I will bike back in a hurry." I smiled. I watched as my grandmother chuckled at my remark.

"Give your little brother a hug from me when you see him!" I nodded and hugged her. When we released one another, I turned and dashed out of the house. Tuesday, the cat, walked up to my grandmother and sat down. She looked up to her.

"I hope Brian won't be a problem."

I rode my bike back to my town following the road this time. I took my time biking back to enjoy the early morning sun and the landscape around me. Being with my grandmother for one week had been refreshing. Biking to school was a bit of a long way, but I coped just fine. As the cars passed by, I wondered how Phillip had coped without me. I know for a fact that if I wasn't cooking for the two boys, they would've just got takeout. I shivered at the thought that Brian was going to ground me again. I wouldn't be surprised if he did, since I had deliberately disobeyed him. Running away from Brian a week ago was the best thing I'd ever done. It gave me a sense of control over my own life. However, at the same time I did feel regret that I had left Phillip alone with him. I hoped he wasn't too strict or mean to him.

My attention shifted quickly to a tall wall near the abandoned school. It was there, standing on the horizon waiting for me to pass. I decided to do something different. I hurried towards the gate and stepped off my bike. I leaned against the wall and locked it. I approached the gate and the young man I saw a week ago stood there staring at me, as if he had been waiting for me to show up. It was like he was expecting me.

*'You can see me then?'* he said. I nodded.

*'And you can hear me clearly?'*

"Yes." I replied.

*'I want to apologize for scaring you the other day. It wasn't my intention. I was in search of someone who could help me.'*

"The 'other day' you're referring to happened a week ago. During that time, I have conquered my fear of spirits and now I can communicate with them. What do you want?" I asked folding my arms across my chest.

*'A week?'* the young man whispered. I looked around for a moment. I felt eyes on me and saw another pedestrian. I smiled at him politely, pointing at a pink flower growing from a crack in the wall. He gave a slight nod and continued on his way. I gritted my teeth.

"It's not safe for me to talk here in public. People will think I'm crazy." I said irritated.

*'I understand, but I need your help, Jeanny. That's all I need from you, your help.'*

"Wait... How... How do you know my name?" I asked astounded. "What do you need help with...?" I watched as the spirit turned around and began to vanish from sight.

"Wait...! Ugh! Figures..." I said frustrated. I looked around for him. Nothing. I shook my head and walked back to my bike. I climbed on it and headed back to Brian's house.

I opened the door to the house, expecting Brian to rush towards me and scream. Instead, Phillip came running up to me and hugged me tightly.

"Why did you leave me?" he said crying. "Don't you love me anymore?!"

"Obviously I do, Phillip, but I needed to see Grandmother. It was getting a bit suffocating in here but it doesn't mean I didn't miss you."

"As I missed you, and Dad is waiting for you in the living room." There was a tone of dread in his voice that caused shivers down my spine. I collected my courage as I nodded and took a deep breath. I patted Phillip's head softly before proceeding into the living room where Brian was sitting on his chair.

I looked at him and waited until he made eye contact with me. I saw that the television was turned off for a change. He turned and looked up to me. "We need to talk Jeanny. You may want to sit down."

"I am good standing here," I said folding my arms across my chest. "I sat long enough getting here and I'm expected at school, so I can't stay long." I shifted my eyes and thought, 'I would love to sit down but not with you in the room.'

"Fine," Brian said letting a sigh escape his lips. "Look, I know we got off on the wrong foot in regards to your treatment…"

"If this has got to do with me seeing a doctor or, let's use the proper term, shall we? Psychiatrist or psychologist. I'm not going. Heck, you might as well send me to a demonologist and analyse whether I'm truly possessed by a demonic entity."

"Jeanny, please just listen…"

"No, you listen to me." I pointed at him. "I stayed at my grandmother's house for a while and she told me how you ditched Mother because of her gift. In other words, you didn't care enough to accept her for who she was."

"Don't you dare say that to me. I loved your mother more than you know!"

"Obviously not enough!" I said raising my voice. "I am fully aware you provide for all of us in financial terms, but we've hardly had any time to grieve together. You lock yourself up in your bedroom late at night, drinking beers and watching the game. When did we ever go out to a park like a normal family? It would've been something Mother would've wanted us to do, but no, I have to slave around here in the house to keep up with the laundry, cooking and taking care of Phillip whilst you sit there day in and day out, going to work and going home, you make yourself too comfortable. You sit there daring to take me to a professional to analyse my mental state?! How dare you treat me this way!" I turned around absolutely fuming. I balled my left hand into a fist and squeezed it so hard it turned white.

"Jeanny! Stay here! We are not done talking!" Brian said as he rose from his chair. I knew he was following me and I hurried out through the front door. I knew Phillip must've been in the kitchen or the dining room peeking around the corner when I confronted Brian, but he must've understood why I had to burst out the truth like this... Or was I too harsh?

I got on my bike and rode as fast as I could away from the house. I hurried down the street, expecting to hear rapid footsteps behind me, but nothing. I looked back and saw Brian standing in the doorway shaking his head.

I hurried back to school to submit the assignments that had been given to me through the mail a day or two after Marion had spoken to the school over the phone. I knew my grade was going to be affected by my attendance; however, my grandmother thought it was just a council thing to keep children in check. She said as long as I kept up with studying and submitting assignments, there wasn't really a problem about not being physically in the classroom. She explained that even students at universities did the same thing; they wouldn't show up for class, but as long as they did the assignments and worked ahead, most were fine.

I reached the front of the school reception and asked where I should drop off my assignments. The receptionist explained that the principal wasn't in because he had a meeting that day, but she was happy for me to proceed to my classroom and drop off the assignment to my teacher. I followed her instructions and walked to my classroom.

The dread in my stomach started to build up as I got closer to my classroom. It was occupied and in session. Samantha was in class and we hadn't seen each other since the café. I gathered up my courage and knocked on the door.

*"Come in!"* a female voice said. I grasped the handle of the door, turned and opened it. The room went quiet and

everyone redirected their attention to me as I stepped in. I wandered confidently to the teacher and passed her the plastic folder with my assignments in. She took it appreciatively and opened it. She pulled out the documents and went through them thoroughly.

"Sit next to me," she asked me. I nodded, pulled a chair from a small room behind her and sat down. The teacher looked at the other students as they kept staring at me.

"Get back to work," the teacher said firmly. As she said that, the students looked back to their work.

"I am happy with the work you've done so far," the teacher said. "How is the research for your presentation going?"

I sighed. "I need more time off school to work on the presentation and the essay. I need to interview some people who were actually there when the tragedy happened."

"That's fine," the teacher said. "Don't worry about automated letters coming to your house. I know it can be extremely intimidating when they say your attendance is in 'jeopardy'. However, I know you're a good student and you care for your education, so continue your research and do the interviews for the presentation."

"Alright, thank you." The teacher handed me a folder with my assignments for the next few weeks. I suspected they needed to be done.

"I'll see you next week," the teacher said. I nodded and got up. I said my goodbyes to the teacher and hurried out of the classroom.

I felt Samantha's staring me as I left. She had probably kept her obnoxious gaze upon me hoping I would acknowledge her. Unfortunately, I didn't care much for her anymore.

I hurriedly left the premises and cycled my way back.


I placed my bike against the fence at my grandmother's house. After locking it and heading towards the door, a young boy around the age of 14 snatched my backpack and ran down the street.

"Hey!" I yelled out. I ran after him. Behind me, I heard the door open. The boy ran around the corner and I followed closely behind.

"Jeanny!" I heard my grandmother yell but I was focused on the boy. I saw him run into an alleyway while I was only a few feet behind him, trying to avoid the oncoming pedestrians that slowed me down. The alleyway was a dead end. He stopped in his tracks and looked around in panic. I approached slowly once I had caught up to him.

"You're cornered. Just give me the backpack back and I won't report you to the police." I extended my hand so he could hand me my backpack. Instead, he fumbled in his pocket and pulled out a knife before pointing it at me.

"I can't do that," he said. "I need your money."

"Look, I'm a 16-year-old schoolgirl. I don't even have a job to earn enough money to rent out an apartment. Why would you want to steal money from a student?"

"You wouldn't understand! I have to!" the young teenager said shakenly. I moved closer to him.

"Look, whatever or whoever forces you to steal from other people, it's your choice not to. Nobody can force you into anything. Please, young man, just give my backpack back, please."

"No, I can't! I have to give it to her! My name is James!"

"James, huh? Whom do you need to give it to?" I asked. I was hoping I could talk some sense into the young man so he would give me my belongings back. My notebook with all the notes for the book that I'd started to write were in that backpack.

"It doesn't matter who! I just have to do this... Please move aside." I looked at him and saw he was shivering with the knife in his hand. A sigh escaped my lips as I stared at him. I slowly took off my jacket and went into a defensive stance.

"I won't step aside, James. I have items in that backpack that nobody else could want. If you want to pass, you'll have to go through me first."

"Have it your way then!" he yelled tossing my backpack aside. He firmly held onto the knife in his hand and dashed towards me. I moved aside missing the sharp edge of the knife, and kneed James in the stomach in a swift motion. He grunted and cringed from the pain. I made sure there was enough distance between us as he regained his composure and attempted to slash me. He moved forward swaying the knife dangerously in front of him. I had no choice but to step back to avoid his continuous assault. I quickly looked behind me to see if there was enough room for me to manoeuvre or if there was anything available for me to use against him. I spotted a long piece of lumber and swiftly grabbed a hold of it. James dashed towards me with his knife. I managed in the last second to block his slash attack. I swung the piece of lumber at his head. He ducked. I was glad there was some distance between us when I swung at him again. This time he moved to the side. I took the opportunity to kneel and swipe at his legs, knocking him off his feet. He fell backwards to the ground landing back first. His knife fell out of his hand. Throwing the lumber out of range, I hurried to his side, kicking the knife out of arm's reach. I watched as James attempted to crawl away from me towards my backpack. I grabbed hold of him and used my weight to hold him down onto the ground. He grunted.

"Get off!" he yelled. I grabbed his arm and locked it aggressively behind his back. He winced in pain.

"Stop! Please! Let me go! I'm sorry!" he shouted. I knew he was in pain but I had to secure my own safety first. I helped him up and pushed him towards my backpack.

"Grab my backpack," I said sternly. I watched as James leaned down in agony and grabbed the bag with his free hand.

"Please… Whatever you do… Don't get the police involved! Please I beg you!"

"I feel like I should. You tried to rob and assault me. Walk!" I said nudging his back and holding onto his arm. We headed out of the alleyway and went straight to my grandmother's house.


I pushed James and my grandmother stood in the hallway. She had her arms crossed in front of her chest.

"Who's that?" my grandmother asked.

"A thief. He tried to steal my backpack," I said closing the door behind me.

"Your backpack? You got everything?" she asked.

I nodded. "He wanted to steal school books." My grandmother glared at him. James didn't say anything. I guided him into the living room and forced him to sit on the couch. My grandmother approached him.

"Why were you trying to steal my granddaughter's things, young man?" James looked from my grandmother to me before looking back. He didn't reply.

"You better reply otherwise we WILL get the police involved," I said threateningly.

"Okay, alright," James said raising his hands. "I have to steal okay? I have to steal otherwise my sister will kill me for disobeying."

"That is just wrong," I commented scoffing. James looked directly at me after I said this. I made eye contact with him. "It is wrong. I have a younger brother myself, but even if we were in desperate need, I wouldn't want to pull Phillip down. I would just want the best for him."

"D... Does he look up to you?" James asked.

I nodded. "He does and I am proud he looks up to me as an example for him." I watched as James nodded lightly.

"I can't really look up to my sister, you see..." James began, "our father is dead and my mother's an alcoholic. She kicked us out of the house and we had to live on the street. My sister is depending on me to provide her enough money for drugs..."

"What is your name, young man?" my grandmother asked.

"James..." James replied softly.

"I know you're feeling guilty for stealing my granddaughter's backpack, but would you like something to drink and perchance some sandwiches or biscuits?" My grandmother asked.

James perked up. "You would offer me food even after what I've done?"

"You may be a thief, but you were made into one, and not by your own decision." my grandmother explained. "Don't worry yourself too much. I'll make you a warm hot chocolate and some sandwiches."

"Thank you…" James whispered.

"I have to ask, James… Did she start using drugs before or after you were kicked out?" I asked frowning. I sat down in front of him on the floor.

"She started way before. It started with smoking a little marijuana. I asked her why she'd start doing something this illegal and she explained that she just wanted to escape the nightmares we were going through every day," James explained. "You see, my sister was mistreated by our mother day in and day out. I hid in my room the majority of the time when I heard them argue. At some point, my sister decided to do class A drugs like cocaine and heroin. I knew she was only doing them to escape the real world, but it made our family collapse into pieces," James said lowering his gaze. I gritted my teeth. It was terrible to find such a young teenager in this difficult situation.

"Have you ever thought of convincing your sister to go to rehab?" I asked carefully.

James shook his head immediately after my question. "No point. She refuses to stop. Last time I asked her if she would even consider stopping taking all these drugs, she kicked me around like some sort of human ball. I haven't asked her since."

My grandmother walked in the room and placed a tray of food and drink on the couch beside James. "Here you go. Dig in. you must be famished."

"I am…" James whispered. "Thank you so much for your hospitality and generosity. I am so sorry that I tried to steal your backpack…"

I gave him a little smile. "Hey, we know why you did it. I appreciate your apology, thank you."

"Are you still wanting to involve the police…?" James asked vigilantly. I looked over to my grandmother.

"Young man, I won't report you to the police, but you'll have to do something in return." my grandmother said.

"And what would that be...?" James asked with a mouthful of biscuits.

"I want you to live with me and have a normal life. You living on the streets being mistreated by your own sister for her own gain is not right. I'll let you stay with me and even send you to school."

"I... I can't," James said. "I can't leave my sister out there..."

"She's dragging you down James..." I commented harshly. "She will drag you down until you starve and die, all in the name of drugs. Losing your life for something so addictive or ending up in prison, it isn't the way to live your own life."

"It must be hard to let her go..." my grandmother began, "...but it is time for you to think of yourself, to think what you want to do with your life."

"In all honesty, I wanted to become a veterinarian but I haven't been to school for a few months..." James admitted, "and I'm not on the system either..."

I looked over to my grandmother and she approached James, placing a warm gentle hand on his head. "I would adopt you in a heartbeat."

# Chapter 9

'*Can Jeanny please come to the principal's office?*' the speaker announced across the school. There was a pause. '*Can Jeanny come to the principal's office?*' I looked over to James before redirecting my gaze to the teacher. I got up and began to walk out of the classroom. I felt the stares of my classmates. Some were judgemental, some were concerned and some simply didn't care. I opened the door to my classroom and exited. As I entered the hallway, it was quiet. All the students were in their classes studying and learning. I remembered walking down the hallway with my mother. She always used to take me to school. Other children would laugh at me for not being independent but I was glad my mom took time from her writing to bring me to school.

Some laughed at the idea of my mom being a writer, some of them through it was inspirational for someone to pursue their dreams. I know I wanted to publish her books. It was the right thing to do. All her written and artistic works were mine given to me in her will.

I walked towards the centre of my school. The principal's office was on the second floor. I climbed the stairs with thoughts rushing through my head about why the principal might want to see me. Was it because of the school days I'd missed? I would be upset too if an A student began to skip classes; not that I considered myself an A student. I knew I wasn't. I knew I only did what I had to as a student. I may have done my best but apparently it wasn't enough.

I reached the top and saw the principal's assistant sitting there on the phone through a small glass window, perhaps speaking to another parent. She seemed rather stressed. I walked up to the door, took a breath and entered. The assistant noticed me, looked up and pointed at me to go on ahead to the principal's office. I gave her a nod of recognition and walked past her to the office door. I grasped the handle of the door and knocked two times.

"Come in!" said a deep voice. I pushed the door open and it revealed a large office. I looked down into the room seeing the principal, Brian and another woman I didn't recognize.

"Principal Serpentin…" I began, "You wanted to see me?"

"Ah yes. Please, take a seat," he offered. He pointed at an empty chair across from him. I stared at the chair.

Folding my hands together and resting them before me, I replied, "I prefer to stand, thanks." I stared at Brian and wondered why he was here.

Suddenly, a strange uncomfortable thought struck my mind; 'Have they called me in because Brian thinks I'm ill when I fled to my grandmother instead?'

"You'd rather stand?" the principal asked.

I nodded. "Yes. I just came out of my classroom, sir. I'm stretching my legs." I watched as the lady wrote down some notes on a clipboard.

"Your father here thinks you're in need of mental evaluation," the principal began. I scoffed under my breath with disbelief. He was plainly ridiculing the situation. My scoff was clearly too obvious as the lady wrote something else down.

"What does he think needs to be evaluated?" I asked.

The principal looked over to Brian. He, in return, pointed at me. "She's been having hallucinations about spiritual and demonic entities." I raised my eyebrow.

"Is this true?" the principal asked. I kept staring at Brian. He gestured for me to speak.

"She's been skipping classes because of it," Brian added.

I stood there emotionless; however, my heart was raging at the man. It wanted to scream at him but I composed myself. Instead, I replied, "I admit I have been missing classes; however, I have been fulfilling the assignments sent to my grandmother's house and my teacher. I have had my bad days but I don't recall seeing ghosts or what is it called? Demonic what? I don't know what you're talking about. I've been missing classes for a few reasons, sir." The principle watched me intently and nodded for me to proceed.

"I have been doing outside research for my end-of-year presentation and I also skipped school because of my boyfriend... sorry... my ex-boyfriend. He left to live in Australia. With all of that, I couldn't always find a way to cope with my emotional distress and so I've been finding other ways to focus on my assignments and research."

Brian shook his head. "She's denying everything."

I looked over to the principal with concern on my face. "I'm worried about him. He hasn't been acting himself lately. He consistently sits in front of the television drinking beer after beer and isolating himself from me and Phillip.

I'm practically raising my brother alone." I watched the lady writing down notes as I spoke. Brian stuttered.

"Is this true?" the principal asked.

"I… Eh…"

"Don't get me wrong…" I continued, "ever since the death of our mother, he's been going downhill. Quite frankly, we're concerned about his wellbeing. I think my 'father' here is the one needing mental evaluation…" I paused before adding, "And I'm not proud that I've been skipping school or missing classes, but losing something I thought I loved knocked out my ability to concentrate on school. It hurts returning to school when I can't see him. I'll say sorry again for skipping classes and I'll try my best to catch up on the curriculum for this year."

The principal stared at Brian with disbelief, "I can't believe we pulled an A student from class for a psychiatric evaluation when the problems lie with you, Mr. Trevaros." I acted surprised as the principal mentioned the real reason for pulling me out of class.

"Jeanny, please return to your class. I apologize deeply for the inconvenience. I hope you haven't lost any precious time from the lesson."

I nodded. "Alright." I turned away from them and began to walk out of the office. Brian was protesting behind me but I didn't wait to pick up the nonsense he was spitting at them. One thing I remembered from my mother at a young age, was, don't let psychiatrists know your problem, for when you start to tell the truth about your thoughts or any spiritual relations, they'll think you're insane or mentally challenged.

I exited the office and stared at the assistant again. She was busy with another phone call. My thoughts of my mother were bothering me. When she first discovered her own connection with the spiritual world, Brian would've sent her off for a mental evaluation. Because they didn't understand the spiritual aspect, they deduced she was insane and wanted to book her into an asylum. Brian, however, didn't go through with the idea of sending her away but was severely concerned nonetheless.

I returned to class and all the other students stared at me when I returned to my seat. As usual, I ignored their stares as I nodded at my teacher, refocusing my attention on my assignment.

James and I walked down the hallway of my school as the bell rang. Some students greeted us happily as I turned to James. He had been living with us for about a week now and looked like a completely different person, since my grandmother had given him new clothes, school supplies and placed his name on the system. They didn't mind him being under her care until further notice. I did notice however, that James was extremely exhausted from answering questions from the social workers' team. They were repeatedly asking the same questions and getting the same reply from him. It was like they weren't paying attention to any of the words from his lips.

"Did you enjoy your week at school?" I asked him.

He nodded with a smile. "Yes. I'm happy. I'm so happy your grandmother accepted me in her home, but I'm wondering what would happen if my mom was searching for me, or worst case, my sister."

I grabbed his shoulders firmly but not enough to hurt him. "Come on. If anything happens, I am here for you. I'm not going to let your mother or your sister abuse you over a dose of cocaine or a bottle of whiskey. You don't deserve that. You have the opportunity now to chase your dream.

You've made some nice friends here in only a few days. Why would you want to throw it away?"

"I know. I don't want to go, but my mom and sister need me. I can't just abandon them."

"What? By stealing for them and ending up in prison? If you're in prison, you can't help them," I explained. He looked down. I knew he was disappointed but I'd made a rather valid point that he should stay and pursue his dreams. "I don't want to be the bringer of bad news, but people like your mother and sister, they won't change for anybody else. They'll only change if they choose to."

"I suppose you're right…" James said still staring at the ground. I felt bad for him, but for some reason I wanted to see him succeed. I guess it was my sisterly affection kicking in.

"Come on James. Let's go back home," I said patting him on his shoulder. He nodded and I knew he wasn't happy, knowing he had to think of his future first and abandon his family.

I couldn't even begin to imagine how brave he had to be and how much emotion he'd have to battle to pursue his dreams. We walked towards the school gates, when I spotted a group of young adults smoking there. I'd never seen them around the school before and a sensation of unease overwhelmed me. I shifted my gaze towards James. He had noticed the group as well and he slowed down his pace and began to hide behind me.

"She's here…" James said whispering. "She found me…" He began to shiver in fear as I watched a girl of about 18 or 19 walk towards the gate.

"Who?" I asked, but I knew who he meant.

"My sister Kim… Please help me." I grabbed my phone and shoved it in James's hand.

"Dial the police in case something happens." I wondered how in the hell the sister knew where my school was, unless of course she had spies following him wherever he went.

"Hey, James! I've been looking for you! Where's the money?!" the young woman said loudly across the courtyard. James shook his head.

"I don't have anything…" he whispered.

"You little shit! Don't shake your head at me! Where's the money!" the young woman yelled.

"Hey! Leave him alone, you bully!" I exclaimed walking towards the gate. James stayed long way behind me as I stared at her firmly.

"Who are you?" she asked.

"Someone who doesn't tolerate abusive behaviour," I said sternly.

"You want me to smack that pretty face of yours?" she snapped.

"I'd like to see you try," I said crossing my arms in front of my chest, "but I'm warning you. I've got the police on the phone." James's sister Kim stared at me with hate-filled eyes.

"Keep that mutt then." She turned and began to walk away. I made my hands into fists and clenched them so hard they turned white.

"You know. I pity you," I said, unfolding my arms. Kim stopped in her tracks. I could see the baggy rings under her eyes and her clothes had seen better days.

"What did you say?" she screeched.

"You've got such a sweet young boy for a brother and you treat him like shit. You as his older sister should be

167

an example to him. Someone he can look up to," I said. Kim turned back and walked up to the gate. I opened the gate to let the young woman enter.

"Bitch! You have no idea what you're talking about," she said shoving her finger close to my face as if she was trying to lecture me.

"Actually, I do. It's just so sad to see someone like you not worthy enough to have a sibling in their lives."

"You know nothing, you fat ass bitch!" Kim shouted.

"Do you really think petty insults will get you anywhere?" I asked. "As far as I'm concerned…" I was cut off from my sentence when Kim lunged at me. I managed to step aside and planted a knee in her stomach. She cringed in pain, holding onto her stomach. I quickly leg-swiped her and she fell backwards onto the ground.

"Hey! What's going on here?!" a male voice exclaimed from behind me. It was one of my teachers.

I took a few steps back, raised my hands and replied, "Just a drugged girl looking for trouble, sir. She trespassed on school grounds without permission. I only acted in self-defence when she lunged at me."

"Yes, I saw. Get home, you two, before I send you to the principal's office." I lowered my hands, nodded and hurried over to James, grabbing his hand. I pulled him towards the bike stands that were on the opposite side of the main gate and grabbed our bikes. I turned to see my teacher grabbing Kim by the arm helping her back to her feet. The group Kim was with quickly dispersed as the teacher threatened to get the police involved. Another teacher had arrived and kept Kim under control in the school's courtyard. She was screaming, crying and cussing trying to fight out of the adults' grip. I suspected that they were going to report the incident to the police. I wouldn't be surprised if I received a phone call or letter to file a report for the police. James and I hurried out of the school's courtyard and tried to get some distance between these young adults and ourselves, wherever they may be.

As we were biking our way back to my grandmother's, I decided to bring us to the abandoned school's wall as a quick pitstop to take a quick breather with James.

"Why'd you bring us here?" James asked, noticing the menacing foliage that had dominated the concrete wall.

"I'm sorry, it's complicated to explain," I said stepping off my bike.

"Jeanny, I don't like this place." James said as he cautiously looked around.

I nodded and placed my hand on his shoulder. "I know. I don't either, but I need to do something really quickly."

"If you don't like being here, why did you bring us here?" he asked. I shrugged and took a moment to think. *Why indeed did I bring us here?* I looked around and couldn't find anything suspicious.

"Wait here for a minute, James…" I said. "I'm just going to check something."

"Please hurry…" James whispered.

"I will," I reassured him. I wandered along the wall until I reached the gate. There the young ghostly figure stood waiting for me.

*'You've come back,'* he said with an echoey voice. It gave me shivers down my spine.

"You pulled me towards this school, didn't you?" I asked.

The young man shrugged. *'Perhaps, but it doesn't take much persuasion or manipulation to have someone do what you want when the grain of curiosity has already been sown.'*

"Whatever the purpose or aid you seek, I cannot provide any at the moment. I have more important matters to attend to," I said sternly.

*'That will have to wait...'* the young man said, turning around. I stared at him with disbelief. Did he just ignore me?

*'I need you to follow me somewhere more private,'* he said. I watched as he began to float away from me.

I shook my head and firmly shouted after him, "You can wait!" I turned around and wandered back towards James. I closed my eyes briefly before opening them again. There he was, the young man's spirit staring at me menacingly.

*'Where do you think you're going?'* he snapped.

"Like I said: I can't provide any help for you at the moment. You'll have to wait until I can sort James out," I said explaining.

171

'I have been trying my utmost best to keep you safe, Jeanny,' the young man said. 'I don't know for how long, but you have to help me as soon as you're able. Please, Jeanny, I'm begging you here...'

I sighed, frustrated. "We only have one life here, you know. We have to use it wisely. Please enlighten me as to why yours is so much more important?"

'Trust me... you will not have a life if you do not help me,' he said. I frowned at him as he began to dissipate. I shook my head and walked towards James.

He tilted his head and asked, "Are you okay, Jeanny? You've been acting a bit weird..."

"What do you mean?" I replied knowing fully well that James was not aware what my grandmother and I had in common.

"You were just staring at nothing but talking out loud," James said.

"Don't worry about it," I reassured him. "I tend to talk to myself a lot." I took a moment to look at him. He didn't appear convinced.

"It looked like you were talking to 'someone'," James said.

"Look, I'm trying to write a book and the only way to organize all these thoughts is to go somewhere that inspires me and talk to myself. I'm trying to get my mind into my character," I explained, "So yeah, it kind of looks like I'm talking to someone when I'm actually talking to myself."

"Ah... I think I understand," James said. He seemed a bit more reassured when I gave him that little white lie.

"Writing a book is hard," I added. "Let's not dwell on that though. Let's return back home." James sighed, relieved as he climbed on his bike. I did the same. I looked back one more time towards the gate and the school before biking away with James.

We arrived back in the city after a long bike ride. I watched as James rode ahead of me. I could tell that he was eager to go back to my grandmother Marion's house. I wasn't surprised after his sister dared to show her face at our school. I began to ponder about what may or may not have happened to Kim. The police may have picked her up and put her in a cell overnight after assaulting a student and trespassing on private property. I shook Kim and my worrying thoughts about her out of my mind when, suddenly, I heard a group of male voices behind us. I turned my head to look and saw two or three familiar faces I'd seen standing by the school biking and running after us.

"Pedal quicker, James!" I yelled out. James turned his head and looked at me. I could see the rising fear in his eyes as he whipped his head back and began to pedal quicker.

"Come here, you bitch!" one of the guys yelled out.

"Whatever you do, James! Don't look back!" I shouted. I could see James pedal even quicker as he turned a corner. I followed him close behind as we knew we were at least five minutes away from my grandmother's house.

"Give us what you owe us!" another male voice exclaimed. I didn't reply to them and my phone was in James's pocket. It was a pain that I wasn't able to get to it. Up ahead, I managed to see James jump off his bike and run inside the house. I sighed with relief. I turned my head to look behind me and saw the group of guys still close on my arse. I redirected my attention to what was ahead when a car came around the corner. I barely missed the vehicle, lost control of my bike and fell off. Damnit! I thought as I rolled across the concrete of the sidewalk. The car stopped and the driver stepped out. The group of guys managed to catch up to me and dragged me to my feet.

"Now we got you!" one of the guys said. My mind was still reeling from the fall when I glared at him dead in the eyes.

"Where is that little twerp?!" another guy said.

"Miss, are you alright?" the driver asked as he saw me being surrounded by the group of young adults.

"She's fine!" a third guy said, "Our little sister here was just being clumsy as always. I'm sorry for the inconvenience." I glared at the third guy with a passion of fire. I wanted to burn the guy until his skin melted like Swiss cheese. No words came from my mouth as the driver hesitantly walked around his car to see if there was any damage to the paintwork. Nothing. The guys that surrounded me held me close with their hands wrapped tightly around my arms as they watched what the driver was doing. Seeing no damage done, he wished us all a good afternoon and got into his car, driving away. My heart sank to the ground in horror as I watched him leave.

"Now we are alone," the first guy said dragging me down the street with the guys following close behind. I glimpsed quickly at my grandmother's house and saw her standing by the window. She had the phone to her ear and a blast of relief made me feel stronger. *The police are on their way.* I said to myself. I watched as the guys dragged me into a small alleyway nearby. They pushed me towards the ground. I stumbled and fell onto the hard concrete floor where there was shattered glass, old newspapers and soaked cardboard everywhere. I heard the guys laughing as if I had fallen into some sort of sick prank of theirs. I raised myself slowly as one of the guys approached me. He grabbed me by the hair and I whimpered in pain.

"Where is that little pipsqueak?" he asked. "If you tell me we won't have to put bruises and cuts over that pretty face of yours."

I chuckled a little which caught the guy off guard. "It must be so satisfying to threaten a girl younger than you," I commented. "It must be making you so brave and manly to gang up on a minor."

"Shut up, bitch," the guy said. He raised his hand and slapped me across my face. It made my cheek sting a little but I heard some of the guys whisper to one another. It was obvious that some didn't agree with this guy's treatment.

"Where is that little runt with our money?" the guy said threateningly. "I won't ask you again. If you don't give me an answer, I'll do more to you than slap your pretty cheeks." He pulled me up by my hair and I winced in pain.

"Tell me!" he said, raising his voice.

"I won't tell you shit," I said to him. He yanked my head back as he pulled out a knife and pressed the cold blade against my skin.

"It's such a pity to cut this beautiful fair skin of yours, but you're not leaving me any choice."

"Hey come on, man, this isn't the way to do this," a second guy said.

"We can find that little runt without her," a third guy said.

"Let me have my fun!" the first guy said. "Just stand watch!" I didn't hear any response from the other guys, which was a bit concerning. Had they left the alley? They left me alone?! With him?!

"Oi! Did you hear me?!" the first guy said turning his head towards where he thought his group of friends were. From the corner of my eyes, I saw three or four sets of legs

177

wearing dark trousers unlike any that the guys I'd seen previously had been wearing. I could just about recall them wearing sweatpants with patches and holes.

"Drop the knife!" a stern male voice said. I was yanked onto my feet and pushed in front of the guy as a shield. I managed to see four police officers, two of which held tasers in their hands.

"Drop the knife, sir! We won't ask you again!" the first officer exclaimed.

"Miss are you alright?" another officer asked. I gave a slow blink as an indication that I was alright.

"I won't let her go! You will let me pass!" the guy behind me said trying to assert his dominance over this hostage situation.

"Sir, there will be no negotiation." the first police officer said. "Your mates have been arrested and there is no way for you to escape this alleyway. If you kill the hostage, there'll be a few decades waiting for you in prison. Do the right thing and release the young lady." I stared at the officer calmly. I was quite surprised by how calm I was during this situation. I knew the four officers wouldn't engage unless told otherwise. I felt the blade slowly leave my neck as I wondered what I could do to help the police.

The guy, who still had a hold of my hair, pointed his knife towards them. He extended his arm completely and yelled, "I won't go to jail I've done nothing wrong!" He tried to convince the police that it was my fault and that I'd forced his hand. I shook my head at the absurdity and an idea came to mind. It was risky, however. Luckily, the guy still had the knife up near my head and not right on my neck. I took the opportunity to bend forwards as if pretending to fall. The guy still had a firm grip on my hair and yanked me back but before he realized what was happening, I had moved forwards, lifted my right leg and stomped as hard as I could on his toes. I regretted that I wasn't wearing my two-inch heels. They definitely would've left a mark. To my advantage, however, the guy jumped back letting go of my hair as he groaned in pain. I ducked forward somersaulting towards the police to create distance between the guy and me. I stayed low on the ground as the police took control and moved forwards to shield me with their tasers at the ready. Having no shield to protect himself with any longer, the guy tossed his knife on the ground and raised his hands above his head, surrendering to the police. He glared at me as if he truly wanted to kill me. Once subdued and placed in cuffs, I was pulled aside by a female officer asking me if I was alright. I reassured her that I was and gave my full statement in regards to Kim and the group of guys that had been at the school and how they followed and threatened us.

After 20 minutes of giving my detailed witness report, I was hugged by my grandmother who had waited patiently with James at the side-lines. An ambulance was luckily not needed at the scene but I felt bad for them having to come to a non-emergency hostage situation. I suppose it was protocol. The paramedics took a moment to check if I was alright. Apart from small cuts, bruises and a red mark on my cheek, I was alright to go home.

I was escorted back to my grandmother's house with Marion, James and the female police officer. We thanked her before walking into the house. I immediately headed into the living room. My grandmother followed.

"Jeanny, you okay?" she asked. I sat down on the couch and leaned back.

"Apart from encountering Kim, James' older sister, seeing this ghost boy again, insisting that his problems are more important than keeping James safe, and being assaulted by a gang of immature and aggressive young adults who may or may not have wanted to rape me. I'm feeling fantastic!" I exclaimed with mixed emotions.

"Wait a minute…" my grandmother said, "What was that about a young spirit insisting you help him?" She raised an eyebrow.

I shrugged. "He wanted me to follow him. I refused and told him his issues were something I'd solve on another day. I added that James and I only had one life and we had to preserve it. He went on to say that I wouldn't live very long if I didn't help him."

My grandmother shook her head. "You silly child!" she exclaimed. She stormed out of the living room. James was utterly surprised seeing Marion walk out like that.

"Is she okay?" he asked. I looked at him directly and shrugged.

"I don't know. She called me a silly child for whatever reason…" I said.

"The reason for that is that you need to go and see him now!" my grandmother exclaimed walking in with a phone to her ear.

I sat up straight on the couch. "What?!" I said.

"You're going back there to help him." my grandmother said.

"But… Why?" I exclaimed.

"If he says it's a dire situation that requires your attention, I expect you to help him immediately instead of stalling, especially if your own life is at risk."

"I didn't think much of it, Grandmother…" I said. "He wanted me to follow him and didn't give me any context into his problems. You know how spirits are, they give you vague information or pretend to be someone they used to be when they are nothing but a demonic entity to lure you into danger. I'm trying to keep myself safe here…"

"I appreciate the fact that you're being vigilant, but I can assure you right here and now…" my grandmother said sternly, "…That spirit is a genuine spirit that does need your help and he is connected strongly with you and your past."

I looked at my grandmother astonished, "My past?" I said softly.

That caught Marion's attention. "Yes, your past. I didn't mean to bring this up, but that young man is connected to you in that context, yes. You need to see him so you can get answers. I have said too much already as it is."

"Are you telling me that you've been talking to him?!" I asked. My grandmother stared at me and nodded. "Yes, I have to some extent."

I lowered my gaze as I stared at the rug. I heard my grandmother on the phone to what I suspected was a taxi service. James sat next to me and placed his hand on my knee. It sort of comforted me but my mind was swirling with questions with no answers. Who was this guy? How was he ever connected to my past? Was he a family friend or family member? Was it someone that Brian or my mother knew? Either way, my mind raced back to reality when my grandmother walked up to me and said, "The taxi is on its way. Let me get you some equipment to take. Make sure you've got your backpack. You'll need it." She walked out of the living room and went into the kitchen. I got up from the couch and hurried upstairs to my room and grabbed my backpack. I emptied everything out except my water bottle. I grabbed a warm sweater and put it on. I suspected it would be really cold, especially with spirits around. I walked down to where James stood at the bottom of the stairs.

"Do you have to go?" he asked. I nodded but didn't give him any other words of comfort.

"Jeanny!" my grandmother's voice came from the dining room. I followed her voice in and on the dining table were a few items.

"I am giving you these tools to help you on your journey," she said. She handed me a large black long torch, which I suspected could've been from a police officer or security guard. I opened my backpack and placed it inside. She handed me batteries for it, which were quite a bit larger than the regular AA batteries you can buy from a pound store. I placed them in a small pocket in my backpack. She handed me a large box of salt.

"You'll need this in case you need to seal an entity in a room," my grandmother said. I nodded but didn't say anything. As I put the box away in my backpack, my grandmother handed me a necklace. It was a beautiful necklace with an oval gem that had colourations of purple, blue, grey, green, red, yellow and brown.

"This is a labradorite necklace that has been in our family for centuries," my grandmother said. "It will protect you from any negative entities that are present, and help you enhance your ability to see and communicate with entities." I decided to wear it immediately. My grandmother helped me tie it around my neck.

"Make sure you don't take this off," my grandmother said sternly.

"Okay," I said. As she finished, she handed me a black pouch.

"There are a few more labradorite stones in there as well as fluorite. Keep them on you at all times. If you do lose the necklace, at least you'll still have protection on you," my grandmother said. I looked down at the black pouch before touching the necklace with my fingertips. I was amazed how long it has been in the family for.

"Did my mom wear this necklace...?" I lifted my gaze and my grandmother smiled at me. She gave me a subtle nod.

"She wore that necklace with bravery and dignity," my grandmother said. "She always wore it whenever she went out to aid spirits in need." She paused and looked at me. I could tell there was still grief in her heart. Eyes are windows to the heart and soul as they say. There was a pause between us before my grandmother broke the silence.

"I was waiting to give this necklace to you for your birthday, but this seems to be a more appropriate time to make this necklace officially yours."

"Thank you…" I said in response. "It's beautiful."

"Anyway… Back to matters at hand… Here," my grandmother said handing me a tin box which I suspected had food in. I placed it in my backpack and she continued to hand me bottles of water, some soda and a first aid kit. I carefully placed them in my bag.

"Don't forget this. Always have a pocket knife or a multitool with you. You. just be careful, okay?" my grandmother said handing me a multitool. I nodded, placed the multitool in my trouser pocket and went in for an embrace.

"I will," I said whispering in her ear. For a minute, we stood there hugging each other for what felt like eternity. Time seemed to have stopped. When we finally released one another, James came in and informed us that the taxi was waiting outside. I closed the zippers to my backpack and swung it on my back. I walked into the hallway and grabbed my jacket. My grandmother followed me and grabbed her jacket. I looked at her with surprise.

"What? You think I'm letting you go alone in that taxi by yourself to a creepy old school and leave you there to die?" she asked.

"Well... Yeah?" I said in response.

My grandmother started laughing. "You are a silly child, aren't you?" She handed James's jacket to him and said, "Accompany us, young man."

James, confused, reluctantly grabbed his jacket and went to the foyer. My grandmother and I followed him as we exited the house. Locking the front door to the house, James and I got in the back of the taxi. My grandmother quickly followed and sat next to the driver. Giving the driver clear instructions, we were on the road to the abandoned school.

## **Chapter 10**

I stared blankly at the landscape that seemed to zoom by on our way. The sun began to set on the horizon. I checked the time on the taxi driver's radio, 17:49. It was alarmingly quiet in the vehicle. I peeked at my grandmother using the sidemirror of the taxi to see her expression. I could tell she was concerned. I shifted my gaze to James. He seemed nervous and I couldn't blame him. He was pulled into a world he wouldn't believe unless proven otherwise. As the minutes were counting down and we approached our destination, with every mile driven, my nerves began to thicken as adrenaline rushed through me. I wondered what was waiting for me beyond that tall foliaged wall. I closed my eyes and remembered the visions I'd had. Just seeing the images of the state, the school was in, creeped me out. I intertwined my hands before putting them between my knees as I felt them sweating uncontrollably. I kept my eyes closed as I tried to control my breathing. I felt the car slowing down and my head perked up. I looked out the window and there I saw it: the tall wall and beyond that the shadow outline of the school. I peered at the taxi driver. He wasn't feeling comfortable about dropping us off.

"Are you sure you want to be dropped off here?" he asked my grandmother.

She nodded. "Yes. Also, would it be alright to have you stick around? I'll pay you for your time."

The driver drove up to the pavement and stopped. "I'm sorry. You'll just have to call us again if you need another taxi. My shift is ending after dropping you all off."

"I understand, but I'm just an old lady and I can't cope with the cold. It would be greatly appreciated if I could stay in the car with my grandson until my granddaughter has finished what she's come to do. I watched my grandmother pull out her wallet and hand the taxi driver 100 pounds. The taxi driver shook his head and tried to hand it back.

"If you let us stay in the car until my granddaughter comes out, once she's done, I'll give you another 200 pounds for your time and patience." The taxi driver's face went wide with surprise as he nodded and shut off his engine.

"Here we are, Jeanny," my grandmother said. "We'll wait for you in the car, okay?" I sighed and nodded before grasping the handle of the door and opening it. I stepped out of the vehicle and closed it. My grandmother rolled the window down and looked at me. "Be careful in there. There is an evil lurking here and it is hungry…" I widened my eyes as I stared at my grandmother in disbelief.

"That would've been very useful information about 30 minutes ago!" I exclaimed.

"I know, but I also know that you would have refused to leave the house if I'd given you that information," she said with a smile. "Good luck!" She rolled up the window of the car and I sighed heavily. I was annoyed and nervous as I walked up to the gate. I looked back at the parked taxi before I climbed my way over the wall using the gate as leverage.

After I'd landed on the gravel path and continued to go deeper into the courtyard of the abandoned school, I took a moment to take in the scenery. Shrubs and bushes grew from the cracked pavement of the courtyard. Vines grew on the side of the school all the way from the top to the bottom.

"Where are you?" I asked. There was silence. An eerie wind picked up from the west.

*'I am here...'* a faint male voice said. I didn't realize he had appeared behind me. I turned around jumping a bit out of fear.

"Don't sneak up on someone like that! You could make me join you in the afterlife with my heart jumping like that," I said recapturing my breath.

*'I'm sorry. I am glad, however, that you came back at your earliest convenience.'* I nodded but I wasn't that impressed.

"I didn't come of my own free will. You're lucky that my grandmother was kind enough to inform me, an apprentice in the arts, that I needed to help you. You'll have to take it up with her if you want to be grateful," I said. I have to admit, I kind of sounded like a fool answering him back like a spoiled brat.

The male spirit glared at me with his deathly stare. *'Jeanny. Whether you came out of free will or not, I still appreciate you giving your time to this old soul.'*

"Old...?" I commented with a silent scoff. He seemed to have noticed my little comment.

*'Yes. I may not look it, but I have wandered this courtyard for over a decade. I do not know what year it is.'*

"2006..." I said.

*'I would've been 34 then...'* the male spirit whispered. *'Anyway... I need you to follow me to a more enclosed area. Here on the school courtyard is not safe.'* The spirit hovered away from me as I followed him quietly. I noticed that as I passed the building of the school, it was completely dark and black inside. I ignored the feeling of being watched as I hurried to the spirit who waited by the edge of the forest. I was quite amazed how the school had

been permitted to build a sanctuary for students on forest grounds. I watched as the spirit hovered into the forest and followed him silently to a denser area with shrubs and bushes. I had trouble keeping up with the spirit as the branches were tangling in my hair.

*'Be careful. The forest ground can be rather unstable,'* the male spirit said.

"It would've been easier to know this information before entering the forest," I scoffed. "Why is everyone withholding information until the last minute?!" I was annoyed as I felt my feet sink slightly in what I thought was mud, but turned out to be a large patch of moss. I panted and pushed a branch aside in frustration. It came whipping me back on the side of my face as I grunted in pain.

*'You should've been a bit more careful there... Jeanny.'*

"No shit," I said frustrated. There were small branches and leaves sticking in my hair that I wasn't aware of.

"Before you say anything else. I have some questions that need answering," I said in a demanding tone of voice.

*'Fair. Ask away.'*

"You have to tell me who you are and why you desperately need my help. I can't help you if you leave me in the shadows."

*'I do want to apologize to you about that, but I wasn't strong enough to maintain this so-called solid form to communicate with you. It takes a lot of energy to do so.'* I nodded, for I was quite aware that spirits had a limit depending on the amount of energy absorbed.

*'I have been trying my best to absorb as much energy as I am able to muster for this moment,'* he added.

"I understand." I said.

*'My name is Simon and the reason I'm asking for your help is because my other friends are still trapped in that school.'*

"What do you mean trapped?" I asked. For a moment there, I was pondering on his name. Simon. I had to admit that the name did suit him.

*'I'm not sure how to explain it to you. I don't even know if your grandmother has said anything about spirits being trapped or tied to a place.'*

I shook my head. "No… She hasn't taught me anything in relation to trapped spirits. I can't even fathom what to do," I said. "But she did teach me the basics… like if you were a suicide, I might be able to guide you to the other side, but a whole school full of spirits? That's a new level for me… Are you a suicide victim?" Simon shook his head.

*'Look at my clothes. Does that look like anything like suicide? I doubt anyone would've wanted to stab themselves more than three times in the chest.'*

"Hey! A lot of people nowadays actually do commit suicide whether it be by hanging, shooting themselves in the head, drowning themselves or even taking an overdose of different type of drugs, the struggle is real." I cringed as I felt a dose of adrenaline rush through my veins. I began to shake a little. "You were murdered then."

*'Unfortunately, yes,'* Simon said.

"Do you perhaps know who might've been responsible for your death?" I asked.

*'I do… to some extent…'* Simon said.

"But…?" I said because I was certain there was more to that statement.

*'I do not know his name... I only recognize his face,'* Simon added.

"That doesn't help..." I said sighing. I watched as Simon lowered his gaze. I lifted both of my arms to comfort him. "Sorry...! I didn't mean to like..."

*'No... It's alright. You're right. It doesn't help you much to know who murdered me. Besides, my death isn't important right now. There are trapped souls in that school that need to be saved from the tyranny that reigns there.'*

"Are you kidding me right now?! Your death isn't important?! I want to hear your story first," I said in shock.

*'For me, my story is not that important, but if you insist... You might as well sit on that boulder there...'* He pointed at a boulder underneath the tree. I followed his finger and sat on the cold surface of the boulder, watching him carefully.

*'Alright, don't freak out...'* He paused, *'..but I knew your mother...'* I looked at him wide-eyed and dumbfounded.

"Say what now...?" I exclaimed.

'Please... Let me explain,' he said, 'It was an ordinary school day. Me and your mother were walking down the pavement towards the school. We were the best of friends... We grew up together in the same street and our houses were just across from one another. When we were in art class, your mother was a very talented and creative individual. She would be painting on large canvasses while the other students were scribbling in their sketchbooks. If she wasn't in art, she was talented in music and sports. She didn't once complain about the struggle she had to go through with other subjects. She was, in my book, a class A student. I was always there to lend her a hand with the "boring" stuff such as mathematics or physics.' Simon paused for a moment and I became more anxious to know more about my mother. I knew right of the bat that my mother was creative.

'One day, however, when we were in math class, there was a storm brewing on the horizon. It hadn't even been predicted in the weather forecast that morning. We both looked at the thunderstorm through the window from our classroom. The power soon cut off in the school after a lightning bolt struck nearby. The fire alarm went off and the school had to be evacuated. Only a few students fled the premises including me and your mother. We rushed down *the corridors in a calm and swift manner. We exited the building by using the nearest fire door. The doors shut behind us and we saw other students slamming their fists on the glass on all different floors. I remembered how I hurried over to the doors trying to open them. They refused to budge. I asked your mother to find something for me to open the door with. Your mother and another student ran to search for an item. I remembered turning my head back to the trapped students and told them that I was going to get them out. I slammed my fist against the glass panels of the doors but they didn't break. Your mother ran by my side and handed me a pair of scissors. Of course, they weren't like a pry or a crowbar, but they would help with breaking the glass. I grabbed the scissors tightly in my hand and began to stab at the glass. The tip made an impact on the glass but it only cracked. It didn't break. Suddenly, we saw the students inside the school yell in horror. A black mass engulfed them, pulling them away from the doors. I stopped and watched in horror. A bloody hand pressed against the cracked glass. I heard your mother yell. As I was trying to save the students, something had pulled them into this black smoke. The only thing left behind when the smoke subsided was a massacre of blood, bodies and some body parts.'*

"Did that monster kill you too?" I asked. Simon shook his head.

*'By the time we realized that our classmates and other students had been killed, some of the people who escaped the massacre went out to get help. Your mother, however, stayed. We tried to open the door but, before I knew it, she was knocked down to the ground. When I turned to see who had dared to lay a finger on her, I was stabbed with a sharp object. Looking over to your mother and then to my stomach, I collapsed on my knees and they kept stabbing me, hoping I would die a painful death.'* I gasped in shock as I listened to Simon's story.

*'Before I knew who had done it, I woke up to see your mother was gone and the police had found my body and that of the poor students in the school. Since then, I've been lingering outside hoping to find your mother or someone with her gift to help me and the students.'* I looked down in shame. Had I known what I know now, I would've helped Simon in a heartbeat.

"What of the mass murderer who killed the majority of the school?" I asked.

'I can't answer that. I just know that I need you to go into that building and free all the innocent souls from the school. It's the only way,' Simon said.

"And how? Just march up in there? Greet all the spirits and say, 'Hey! The exit is right here! Come and collect your freedom'?" I crossed my arms and rested them in front of my chest. "I'm being serious, there's no way I will be able to free a whole school of spirits."

'There is a way, I didn't want to scare you off but, truth be told, there's a monster in there holding the spirits captive.'

I widened my eyes and exclaimed, "WHAT?!"

'It's not a big deal. Just sneak up to the principal's office, grab the dagger on the desk and stab him in the heart. That's it. He'll never know what hit him!' Simon explained.

"You know this how? I thought you weren't able to enter the school," I asked confused.

'I can't stay in the school too long. I can manifest for maybe 5 minutes or so before I am pulled back outside. I try to help my friends on the inside and they collect enough information about what we're dealing with, but I can't help *them in any other way than to watch them wander about or, in this case, haunt the corridors...'*

"Simon, I'm not sure I can do this... I'm sorry." I got up from my boulder and began to pace back and forth in anxiety.

*'Your mother would've helped me in a heartbeat, Jeanny...'* Simon said. *'She would've helped anyone in need whether they were alive or dead.'*

I glared at him coldly. "I'm not my mother, Simon! I'm not some all-powerful exorcist priest witch that can summon energies to break curses! I'm just an apprentice who's barely accepted the fact that I have powers to communicate with and see the dead!" I stopped in my tracks and rubbed my forehead in stress. "I'm not like my mother, Simon... I'm just afraid that I won't be much use to you... or your friends." I paused and heard whispers coming from the forest.

"What is that sound...?" I asked.

Simon followed my gaze and said, *'They are voices of the past...'* He looked back at me. *'Your mother told me about how the forests are the oldest sanctuaries for spirits and creatures. She explained to me that the trees absorb the energies around them and you can sometimes hear the past echoing. In addition, she would always walk into the forest during recess and place herself down, meditating.'* Simon smiled a little. *'Your mother was at one with her element and she was proud of it. If you heard voices speaking out to you, Jeanny, open yourself to them. Sometimes, they want to tell you something you might have missed.'*

"Okay…?" I said with uncertainty. I walked a few more steps past the boulder and stood just down from what I thought might be a patch of moss. I noticed the sun had now fully gone and the forest began to darken around us. I knew I would have to pull out my flashlight very soon from my backpack. I crossed my legs and closed my eyes. I began to focus on the sounds around me as I heard the whispers pick up again. For some weird reason I managed to feel Simon's energy surging through my veins and it was comforting. Words came to me minutes later with flashes of visions.

When I opened my eyes, I got up and stared at Simon who had been watching over me this whole time. "I need to go back to my house…"

*'I will come with you…'* Simon said. I nodded and gave him a small smile. I was actually glad to have him accompany me. I hurried out of the forest and ran onto the

gravel path of the school courtyard. I climbed up the wall and landed feet first on the hard concrete of the footpath. I peered to look at the parked car and saw my grandmother stepping out of the vehicle.

"Are you done already?" she asked.

I shook my head. "Not yet, but the spirits of the forest told me to return home. Something is pulling me there to reveal a secret." I watched as my grandmother lifted an eyebrow.

"I can't explain it..." I continued. "...I have to do it..."

"Please take James with you..." my grandmother said. "He needs some fresh air and maybe meeting your little brother Phillip will soothe him a bit." I nodded and waited for James to step out of the car. I hurried across the main street towards home.

I unlocked the door to the house and walked into the foyer. Phillip greeted me almost instantly and I introduced him to James who quietly shook Phillip's hand. Brian walked over, crossed his arms and stared at us. "What did I say about bringing boys home?"

"He's not staying long. I'm just here to pick something up," I said.

"I can wait here in the hallway, Jeanny. Just go and grab what you need," James said. I nodded to him thankfully and hurriedly past Phillip and Brian. I went upstairs and walked down the hallway. I opened the door of my room. It felt weird standing in my own bedroom again. I stopped. I traced my steps back and stared at my parents' room. I turned my head to look at the stairs. I heard three male voices talking, I suspected Brian was questioning James and about how we met.

Turning my attention back to the door, I headed towards it. I remembered my mother saying when she was younger, and pregnant with Phillip, that her most trusted belongings were in her old grandmother's wardrobe. At the time, I didn't believe her, for I only saw load of clothes and accessories. Remembering her beautiful hazel eyes, I somewhat believed her. She also told me additionally that the wardrobe hid secrets it would reveal in time, when the truth called out to be unveiled. Something was pulling me towards it.

I opened the door to our parents' room and looked inside. A foul smell engulfed my nostrils so I pulled my shirt up and covered my nose. There it stood, the large dark old ash wardrobe in the corner beside the window. I turned the old rusty key and opened the doors. Releasing my shirt, a soothing perfume came from the wardrobe. A wave of nostalgia engulfed me when I recognized my mother's perfume. I moved some clothes aside that were hanging on the bar. I spotted a cardboard box in the corner and grabbed it. I opened it and stacks of letters lay in the box almost to the brim.

"It must be here somewhere..." I said softly to myself. I grabbed a folded letter from the top pile addressed directly to my mother. I unfolded it and began to read the letter. I gasped in shock and folded it back up. I continued to dig further into the box and found copies of police files about a Simon. A dagger lay silently at the bottom of the box in a plastic container still covered in blood. I placed my hand in front of my mouth. I took one of the police reports and read it softly to myself.

"The main suspect of Simon Partridge's death is Brian Trevaros. We are still intending to interview the suspect for mass murder." I looked at the fingerprints with Brian's name on. I was angry and afraid. I closed the box and took it downstairs.

Brian stood beside Phillip as I came downstairs. I suspected he was eyeballing James who was leaning against the wall with a look of discomfort. I entered the living room carrying the old cardboard box. I saw how Brian's eyes lit up with what I suspected was frustration.

"Where did you find that?!" he barked.

"Phillip! Stand away from Brian!" I said loudly. Phillip looked at me with confusion in his eyes before peering at Brian.

"Why?" he asked.

"Don't you dare!" Brian barked again, this time more aggressively.

"Step away from Phillip... Brian's a murderer. He murdered mom's best friend..." I said. Phillip turned to look at Brian. James began to back away slowly towards the door.

"Phillip!" I called out to him. My younger brother hurried over to me. I could tell James was flabbergasted and pulled out my phone from his pocket. I had completely forgotten that James had my phone on him this whole time.

"All the information in that box is nonsense… I am just a suspect, not the murderer."

"Don't you dare lie to me. You ARE a murderer. You killed Simon! Who else would steal an evidence bag with a blood-covered dagger, a document with all their fingerprints and all the reports from interviews with the suspects and witnesses?!" I said. I knew I was putting myself at risk for telling him that I knew what was in the box. I wouldn't be surprised if the first thing that came into Brian's mind was to murder me too. I watched as Brian stood with his hands clenched into fists. There was a pause in the house. No one dared to move except James pressing a button to speed dial a number on my phone.

"You know what else you've forgotten to tell me?" I said as I heard my phone softly began to dial the number and a faint voice come out of the device.

"You've forgotten to tell me that you concealed the truth of my DNA relating to Simon Partridge. He was my biological father!" I paused. "Is that the reason you killed him?! He tried to save other people's lives and you stabbed him in the gut like some kind of animal!"

"I had hoped the truth wouldn't be revealed… I loved your mother and having that scum of a guy take what should've been mine, I had to kill him!" Brian said glaring at me with bloodthirsty eyes. "Now, you have left me no choice but to kill all three of you."

"Even your own son?!" I said referring to Phillip.

"It matters not. Your mother belonged to me! That Simon should've never impregnated her in the first place! That was my honour and pride! Yet here you are! I raised you as my daughter despite you being the filthy offspring of that nerd."

"You must've been so proud to be the one who stabbed Simon multiple times in the chest and knocked mom to the ground when she wasn't looking" I said remembering Simon's words.

"I don't know how you know about this, but yes, I did! I wanted to be happy with your mother! I loved her and she didn't deserve a low life like your father. It doesn't matter anymore, you three will not live to breathe another word of the truth," Brian spat.

I watched as James lifted my phone over his head. "I wouldn't do that if I were you. While you were threatening and explaining everything that happened, I rang the police and they heard every single word you uttered. If I was you,

I'd run." I watched as Brian glared at me with hatred before cursing and turning to the door. He ran. He slammed the door open and exited the house in a hurry. James placed my phone to his ear and began to give them information about Brian and where he was fleeing to.

"Yes, the suspect has left the house, 374 on Spring Avenue. He's heading Westbound." I watched as James hurried out of the door. "He's heading over to Brewer Street."

I collapsed to my knees as the adrenaline rushed through my veins. I felt like crying but no tears came. Phillip kneeled down and pressed himself against me until we were in a tight embrace. Phillip began to cry and I had to soothe him. James walked in moments later. "The police are coming. They want to talk to you and they want you to hand over the missing evidence..."

I looked up to him, "I can't. I have to help my father. You have to give this to the police." I lifted the box and handed it to James.

He took it hesitantly. "Me?"

Phillip and I released one another as I got to my feet. Phillip pulled at my shirt as I looked at James. "I still have something to do at that abandoned school. Can you call on my grandmother to make sure you guys are safe?"

James nodded and Phillip asked me, "Where are you going…? I need you…"

I placed both of my hands on his shoulders and stared at him. "I know you do… But can you be brave just a while longer? Just go with James and he'll guide you to Grandmother. I'll be back as soon as I can."

"Promise?" Phillip asked.

I smiled softly and grasped his pinkie with mine. "Pinkie promise." My little brother gave a small smile back before James nodded at me and they walked out of the house. I followed them before rushing down the street towards the abandoned school.


I entered the courtyard of the abandoned school. I stopped in my tracks and looked around. "Simon? Are you here?"

Simon appeared before me nodding. *'Yes, I am here.'*

"As you are probably aware, the police are tracking Brian down for the crime of murdering you…" I began and I watched as he nodded. "Additionally… in case you didn't know, there was a document that confirmed that I'm your biological daughter…" I said.

Simon appeared flabbergasted by the news as he hovered back a bit. *'You…? My daughter?'* he whispered, *'You're my daughter?'*

I nodded. "Brian was the one who killed you many years ago… I found a box in my mother's wardrobe that can lock Brian away for a very long time."

*'I don't care about Brian…'* Simon said. *'I just want to know why he wanted to murder me in the first place. I never had any problems with him when I was alive. I never saw him interact with me or your mother when we were at school…'*

"He was envious that you were best friends with my mother…" I began. "He wanted her virginity for himself… I don't know how he knew that you and Mother slept with one another, but that was his motivation to end you. At least, that's what I've theorized after what he said to me."

*'Your mother trusted me more than anyone else…'* Simon said. *'That one night we spent together… I confessed my love to her and she hers… That night, we were inseparable…'* I watched Simon carefully. I could tell he felt

happy remembering that night with my mother but I could also see the pain in his eyes.

"I'm sure other answers will come in due time, but we need to help those other poor souls…" I nodded at Simon and hurried over to the school's door.

## Chapter 11

I began to walk towards a set of doors that were completely sealed. Vines covered the walls and doors. I swung my backpack to the front and pulled out the multitool my grandmother had given me. I searched for the knife and looked at Simon. "Always carry a multitool with you... At least, that's what my grandmother says," I said smiling and winking. I began to cut the vines with my knife. Simon watched with interest. I managed to cut the vines away and tried to open the door. It didn't budge. I took a step back and kicked the door near the lock. It shook but didn't open.

"Come on!" I said, kicking the door once again. It finally burst open.

*'Impressive...'* Simon said.

"Learned a bit of martial arts," I admitted as I kneeled down and took off my backpack. "One of my teachers is a martial arts teacher as well as a survivalist tutor." I took out the flashlight that my grandmother gave me and turned it on. "He taught us how to defend ourselves from robbers, rapists etc."

*'Whoever he is, he taught you well,'* Simon said. I snickered a little as I zipped my backpack closed and got back on my feet.

"Thank you. Anyway, here I go." I slowly stepped through the door and entered the school. I walked a few steps before looking behind me. Simon hovered outside.

"Are you able to come or…?" I asked.

Simon shook his head. *'I can't. It's not letting me.'* I sighed.

"Okay… head to the principal's office, grab the dagger and stab whoever's responsible… yes?" I asked. He nodded again.

"Well… wish me luck," I said and gulped.

*'Jeanny…?'* I turned and looked at Simon. *'Be careful… please…'* I smiled and nodded. I walked slowly down the corridors. A foul stench surrounded me. I had to cover my nose and I struggled to gasp for normal air. I looked around me and to my relief, there were no rotting corpses. I suspected the police had swept through and cleaned out the human remains. I continued down the corridor and peered at rust developing on lockers. Brown spots covered the floor and walls.

"I do hope those aren't blood stains…" I said to myself. I walked up to one blob of brown spots on the floor and softly rubbed the tip of my shoe across it. A brown stain was now visible on my shoe.

"Damnit…" I said cursing softly. I ignored the stain on my shoe as I continued walking deeper into the school. I walked up to a corridor and saw a lot of the doors were open. I decided to investigate and tried to read the small plaques on the door. Some were showing classroom numbers and others were for things like the janitor room or the teachers' break room. Two other doors were marked as the male and female toilets.

"Where is that principal's office…?" I said softly. Two large doors caught my attention and I pushed one of them open. The door began to screech loudly over the floor. The sounds of the door echoed across the corridor and I paused. The echoes were somewhat unsettling and I felt something watching me like a predator stalking its prey. I used my flashlight to shine inside the room where it revealed a large stage with seats.

"This must've been the hall where students would perform or the principal give a speech to the whole school…" I said to myself softly. An eerie wind started to blow behind me. I stepped away from the door and shone my flashlight down the corridor. I assumed that a spirit must've passed by me or maybe it was just a simple breeze. I continued to walk down the corridor finding a flight of stairs that led upstairs.

"I pray that the principal's office is not on the top floor…" I said to myself. I continued down the corridor and found the reception. I walked in and it revealed only a few desks with chairs and the kind of old computers I haven't seen in a while. Paper was scattered everywhere and the cabinet drawers were all pulled open. My heart sank, thinking I had found what I was looking for. I wandered out of the reception area and continued my way down the corridor when, suddenly, a pair of hands grasped my ponytail. I yelped in pain as I was yanked backwards. My flashlight fell out of my hand with a loud thud. Both of my hands reached up to the base of my hair.

"Finally!" a male voice said. I immediately recognized it. "You think you can trick me into surrendering to the police? Not a chance, sweetheart!"

"Get off me, Brian!" I yelped. He pulled me back. "Get off of me!"

"Not a chance!" Brian barked. He pulled me closer to him. He was dangerously yanking my ponytail to the point I was afraid he was going to yank the whole chunk of hair from my head. He was pulling me back from what I suspected was the exit. I was too far into my journey to be forced to turn back now. I began to fiddle in my pockets for my multitool. I quickly chose the knife and pulled it out. I looked at Brian from the corner of my eyes. He was so fixated on getting me out of the school that he didn't pay attention. I grasped the base of my ponytail and felt the hair tie. I reached with the knife and swiftly cut off my ponytail. Brian stumbled forwards with the sudden release of pressure and fell to the ground. I turned and ran down the corridor. I swiftly picked up the dropped flashlight and turned it off. I dashed through a door to my left and grabbed the closest thing I could find to jam the handle. I heard the faint movements of Brian getting back to his feet.

"This isn't over, Jeanny!" he exclaimed. "I am coming for you, Phillip and that little rotten whoreson!"

I stayed quiet as I heard him walking. I closed my eyes. I held onto my flashlight and knife so tightly my hands turned white. Suddenly, an eerily loud deep growl echoed throughout the school causing the whole building to vibrate. Layers of dust fell and I coughed. I heard Brian's footsteps recede. Was he leaving the building? I asked myself. I was too terrified to open the door. I leaned my back against the door and sank down to my knees. I hid my face in my legs and closed my eyes. I placed the knife down and felt the back of my head. No ponytail. I slowly opened my eyes and folded my knife away. I placed the multitool back in my pocket and got back on my feet. I turned on my flashlight and noticed I was in the gym hall. Out of sheer shock, I almost dropped my flashlight as I spotted a whole gym full of wandering spirits who all seemed aware of my presence as they stared at me with their empty gaze. I smiled nervously as I raised my hand slowly. "Ehm… Hello!" I said. I watched as the spirits turned to look at one another; they seemed to be conversing with each other. One spirit, however, approached me. He was definitely younger than Simon. He was short and had semi-long hair that covered parts of his face. Parts of his clothes were ripped as if an animal had feasted upon him as prey.

*'Can you see us…?'* the spirit asked. I nodded. He glared at me coldly. *'Living mortals can't see or hear spirits. You are lying.'*

"No… I can assure you. I can see and hear you," I responded to the male spirit. He seemed utterly surprised as I responded to him.

He backed away and muttered, *'Who are you…?'*

*'Johnny! You shouldn't be talking to strangers!'* a female voice said. I peered to look over the male spirit's shoulder to see a female spirit wandering towards me.

*'Anne! I... Well... I just wanted to have some fun spooking her...'* Johnny said with a tone of disappointment, *'... but she can see and hear us...'*

The female spirit ignored the male and approached me. *'Excuse his lack of sensitivity. He doesn't seem to comprehend how dangerous it may be to have some "fun".'*

"Oh, no... It's quite alright," I responded a bit confused.

*'Tell me why are you here and how are you able to see and hear us?'* the female spirit asked.

"Well... you see. My name is Jeanny and I was asked to help you all by Simon..." I said.

*'Simon? As in Simon Partridge?'* the female asked. I nodded.

*'So, he did manage to find us some help!'* a third spirit exclaimed. I watched as Johnny and Anne glared at him. He hurried towards me, *'I talked to him a few times. He said he had found someone we can trust to set us free. That's*

*her!'* He pointed at me. I looked at him. He was about the same height as Johnny but he had shorter hair and wore square glasses. I thought he would've been considered as a bookworm, nerd or probably an IT person.

"I am sure it must be nice for you all to know you can interact with a living breathing human, but I need to go to the princi..." I was cut off by Anne who hissed at me.

*'Don't say that word!'* She glared at me as if she wanted to rip my tongue out of my mouth.

*'Please forgive her...'* the third spirit said. *'She has a lot of hatred built up in her ectoplasmic form...'*

"May I ask why she hates him...?" I asked carefully.

*'It...'* she hissed.

"Ehm..." I said confused.

*'You want to know why I hate that egotistical snollygoster? It's keeping us like cattle for its own sadistic endless appetite.'* she hissed.

"Understood..." I said. "I'll keep it in mind and be careful..." Anne glared at me as I finished my sentence. It was like she was testing to see if I was going to do anything that might provoke her further.

*'You are foolish to think you can handle this thing on your own,'* Anne said.

*'Jeanny, if you don't mind. I'll be able to show you where the office is. It will, however, be very dangerous...'* Johnny explained trying to swerve my attention away from Anne.

"Oh goody..." I said softly. I watched as Johnny headed towards the door.

*'Follow me,'* Johnny said. He disappeared. I followed by unlocking the door and opening it. I looked in both directions cautiously, not certain if Brian was still in the building waiting and ready to pounce. I turned off my flashlight as the rays of the moon shone through the cracked windows illuminating a path for me. Johnny reappeared in the corridor and gestured me to follow. I entered the corridor and hurried to the spirit's side. We wandered down deeper into the school to where I suspected the stairs to the other floors were. Silence remained between us.

"Are you Simon's classmate...?" I asked to break the awkward silence.

We began to climb the stairs and Johnny nodded. *'Simon was a nerd but he played in the soccer team with me* and my friends. He never stayed around to have fun with us though. He was always hanging around with that creative girl, Phoebe.' I widened my eyes. 'He was really lucky to have a girl like her. Sure, she wasn't the diva princess like Anne who was always trying to be the best of everything...'

"What do you mean?" I asked.

'Anne wanted to date the most popular guy in school. She wanted to be the cheerleader captain. She wanted aces for every class etc. A real pain if you ask me.'

"What about Brian...?" I asked and, as I finished my question, I realized how curious I truly was about Brian, my mother and father. It was like I had stepped into their past but knew nothing other than bits and pieces. I noticed that we continued up the staircase to another floor. I began to wonder how many floors this building truly had.

'Who?' Johnny asked.

"Brian," I said.

'You mean that fat freak? He was pushed and bullied by most of my friends. I didn't want to interact with him because of his weird obsession.'

"Obsession?' I asked.

Johnny nodded again. *'He had a thing for Phoebe. He wasn't a student at our school, but every week he gave her flowers in class and quoted a self-written poem to woo her. She wasn't really happy about it. The only thing that bugged him was Simon. He couldn't stand him for numerous reasons. Simon made Phoebe laugh, was always there for her when she needed help with homework and they were the best of friends. Hell, I imagined those two were soulmates.'*
I frowned. I noticed that we were on the top floor of the school and the walls were covered with a black sticky substance.

*'The office is just down the corridor, that large door to your left. Through that door you'll find IT. Good luck…'* Johnny said. I took a few steps forwards towards the corridor. I stopped in my tracks.

"That's it? You're feeding me to the wolves then…?" I said muttering with disapproval. I turned and saw Johnny had vanished. I gulped in fear.

Mustering all my strength and courage, I began to walk down the corridor and my shoes sank in what I believe was a blanket of sticky goo. I cringed at the sound and felt that every single noise would trigger something. Every footstep I took felt like I was going to set off the next event like in a horror game. It felt like walking on an active mine field. The sounds I made echoed through the hallway like a bat echolocating to seek its prey. It made me uncomfortable as I didn't know what creature lurked within the walls.

I snuck my way towards the door with sticky goo gathering more and more underneath my shoes. It felt like I was dragging something heavy with each step I took. It felt like hours as I finally reached the frame of the large door where Johnny said this creature was housed. I peered to look through the windows but they were covered by the same sticky black goo, a few cracks allowed the moon's rays to penetrate and illuminate my path. I took a deep breath and placed my hand on the door. I pushed it hard. The door budged and it screeched at me like a wild animal the further I opened it. No other light illuminated the room. I snuck my way inside carefully and covered my mouth with my one free hand. Heavy footsteps paced back and forth at the back of the room.

"Trying to sneak your way in unnoticed?" a male voice spoke in a deep and alluring tone. An eerie chill ran down my back as I widened my eyes. The door behind me closed with a thud. I turned my head to see the lock of the door flip. I hurried to the handle and tried to open it. Nothing.

"You can't avoid the inevitable. You will be the perfect soul to devour." There was a pause. "Who are you and how did you come into my sanctuary?" the male voice said, trying to interrogate me. I remained silent. The last thing I wanted was for this man or creature to know anything about me. The unknown entity began to walk into the room I was in. His footsteps became louder and louder heading directly to my location. I backed away but didn't go far. My right heel hit the edge of the door.

"Do NOT be afraid. You are not going to die. Not yet at least. Have a seat," the voice said. I knew he was trying to trick me into trusting him with mind tricks to appear harmless. I heard a chair move and something placed itself on it. Candle lights turned on and I had to cover my eyes momentarily. Once they had adjusted, I peered over to the creature on the chair. I gasped in fear. The entity glared at me coldly with his dull red eyes. The creature had the outline of a man yet was completely covered with this slimy black goo.

"Sit," he said. I moved slowly towards the chair opposite the desk where he was sitting. I quickly looked around and the walls were covered with the same black substance. I glared at the two chairs in front of me. Both of them had dark brown or dark red blotches. I cringed for I knew what those stains were. I sat myself on the one that was least covered and looked at the entity. My flashlight lay on my lap turned off.

"You look rather familiar. Have we met?" he asked. I shook my head in response.

"Pity. It would've been so much more entertaining for me to see the light in your eyes vanish knowing who you are whilst I devour you." I stared at the entity with fear and uncertainty. Suddenly, I felt a slithering motion surrounding my body. Upon further inspection, I saw a black gooey rope tying me to the chair.

"Hey!" I shouted in alarm. I tried to wiggle out of the clutches of the rope but I was too late. The rope tightened itself around me making it impossible for me to escape. I watched as my flashlight fell onto the ground with a loud thud.

"You can't escape my clutches, my dear. Let's talk," the entity said calmly. I continued to struggle with the ropes, which seemed to tighten themselves more whenever I tried to fight them. I sighed in frustration and glared at the desk. There was a dagger resting underneath the stacks of paperwork. I peered at the creature and heard Simon's voice echoing in my mind.

*'It's no big deal. Just sneak up to the principal's office, grab the dagger on the desk and stab him in the heart. He'll never know what hit him.'*

*He looks more like a monster than a principal.* I thought to myself. *Tch... If I die, I'll be the one haunting Simon.*

"Who are you and how did you get in?" the male entity asked once again. I could tell by his tone of voice that he was very intrigued and / or curious about how I managed to enter his empire.

"My name is Jeanny," I said cold and sharp. "The door was open."

"That's impossible. No one can open any of the doors except for me," The entity hissed.

"With a decade passing by like a feather in the wind and the hinges rusting like ice in hot weather, it's easy to break a door," I said.

"A decade?" yhe entity said. "What year is it?"

"It's 2006," I said.

"Hm… The year of the flaming dog," the entity said. "Tell me, my dear. What are you doing here?"

"Oh…!" I said quickly thinking of an excuse, "I'm writing a report as part of my homework about this abandoned school. I've heard a lot of stories about this place and I wanted to investigate and take pictures for my report." I stared at the entity and thought to myself, *Clever, Jeanny… Using your school homework as an actual excuse to see if he is or isn't going to devour you.*

"Hmm…" The entity stood up and placed both its hands on the desk. I clearly saw that he had long scrawny fingers with crooked claws.

"Pictures, eh?" the entity said, "You must be fascinated by what happened to all the students that were trapped here." I nodded quietly.

"Well, to help you proceed with your report, lightning struck the building causing a fire on the top floor. Students ran from their classrooms in a panic to exit the building and most of them burned alive," the entity said. "It was such a tragedy to lose so many students."

I frowned a little. Was he trying to make up with a story to cover who he or it really is?

"So where's your camera?" the entity asked.

"Oh…" I said and cursed myself for not thinking sooner that bringing an actual camera would've been more convincing. "I use my mobile phone to take pictures…" I lied.

"Mobile phone?" the creature asked. "Mobile phones don't have cameras. You're a liar."

"Oh no! I'm not a liar." I said as convincingly as possible, "We're in 2006 not 1990. They have cameras now as well as other features."

"Have they now? May I see this new device you claim to possess?" the entity asked.

"Eh… Sure?" I said until I realized that James still had my phone. I cursed softly. "Eh…"

"Is there a problem?" the entity asked.

"My friend has my phone at the moment…" I said weakly.

"Interesting. Should I devour you now to spare you this embarrassing attempt to lie to me?" he hissed. I gave him a death glare.

"You're not here to write a report, are you?" the entity hissed. I kept quiet for I knew if I tried to defend my case, the creature wouldn't consider the possibility I was truly trying to write a report for school. And anyway, at this rate, with paranormal creatures involved, it was going to be a big thick F for failure.

"It doesn't matter," the creature hissed. "Maybe it's time to put that pathetic Simon Partridge out of his misery." The entity gave me a chilling smile before gliding towards the door. It was such an unnatural sight as the door unlocked and opened. The creature slipped outside into the hallway before the door closed shut behind it. I waited for a moment glaring at the door. There was nothing stirring on the other side. I peered at the dagger in its own metal scabbard. I shifted the chair I was sitting on forwards towards the desk. I knew I wouldn't be able to access my multitool and whip out the knife.

"I hope this works..." I said whispering to myself. I leaned forwards so that my chin rested on the desk. I knew the chair I was sitting on was now on just its two front legs and I had to do this quickly. I reached out as far as I could with my mouth to snatch the handle of the dagger. After a few failed attempts at using my tongue to pull it towards me, with a little difficulty, I managed to grasp the handle tightly between my teeth. With the dagger in my mouth, I quickly peered at the door hoping the handle didn't move. There were no sounds of motion coming from the other side. I plopped myself back onto all four feet of the chair and leaned over to my right hand with the dagger. I noticed that the ropes had tied my hands onto the arms of the chair and my feet to the front legs. I slowly slid the handle of the dagger in my right hand and pulled the scabbard off with my teeth. I turned the weapon towards myself and began to move it back and forth to cut the rope from one side. I spat the scabbard out and shoved it as far under my chair as my feet were able to get it. To my delight, the rope was easy to cut through despite it being covered in this mysterious goop. Was this goop like an old shed skin from a snake but more mud-like? I shuddered at the thought and used my free hand to cut myself free from the chair. I stood up and hurried over to the door. I pulled the handle. It didn't budge.

"Locked... Damn," I whispered. I looked around the room to see if there was anything of use to me. I hurried to the chair and grabbed my flashlight, holding it close to my chest.

"Okay… I have the dagger to kill this guy… The question is how to do it…" I said to myself. I began to pace back and forth in front of the door.

*'Pst! Jeanny!'* A voice said faintly from the other side of the door. I hurried closer to the door.

"Who are you?" I asked.

*'My name is Charles! I'm sorry for not introducing myself earlier but I was there with Anne and Johnny! I'm here to help you!'* I was quite surprised to have a companion helping me. I heard the switch of the lock turn. I looked up to the lock and the door slowly opened.

*'There you go! Run whilst you can!'* Charles exclaimed. I shook my head.

"I can't. I need to kill him first. The only way I can achieve that is to stay in here," I said.

*'And do what?'*

"I have a plan, but it needs all of you to make it work," I said with a confident smirk.

## Chapter 12

I sat quietly on the chair with my hands on its arms. I sighed and tried to regulate my heartbeat. I could feel it pounding against my chest as if to tell me I was putting myself in danger doing this. *'I just hope Simon is staying away from that monster…'* I thought to myself. I closed my eyes and prayed he was safe. Moments later, the door opened with a loud screech and the creature glided in.

"That door you mentioned, it was kicked down. Did you do that?" I shrugged my shoulders just a little bit to create the illusion I was still tied to the chair.

"It doesn't matter. What does though, is that I couldn't find that twisted sleazebag anywhere." The creature wandered towards me and placed the gnarled claws of his long-crooked fingers under my chin. It stared at me with its dull red eyes that didn't see my flashlight and dagger.

"What I have been pondering since you entered my office, is how similar you look to a student of mine. Phoebe is her name."

"Oh really?" I said coldly, firmly gripping the weapons with all my might.

The creature gave me a chilling smile. "Indeed."

"Maybe because I am her daughter!" I said spitting at it. "Phoebe and Simon are my parents and there is no way I will let you kill me for your amusement!" The creature began to laugh hysterically which made it close its eyes giving me enough time to leap forward from the chair and stab it with the dagger. I had hoped it would've pierced its heart, but to no avail. I missed. It yelped in pain stumbling backwards.

"Why you!" it hissed. I screamed and stabbed at it again hitting it with the blunt part of the flashlight across its head. Stunned to some degree, the creature raised its hand in an attempt to strike me. I managed to dodge his counter attack by a few inches. I hurried towards the door which still stood wide open.

"It's no use!" the creature hissed. "There is no chance for you to escape…" The door began to swing shut but I managed to slip through at the last second. I heard the creature screech out in frustration as the door closed behind me with a loud thud. Finally escaping the room, I held the dagger tightly in my right hand, and began to run down the corridor towards the staircase. A black liquid substance dripped from the blade onto the floor. I could hear the screeching door behind me open. I was fortunate enough to have reached the stairwell so quickly and began to descend as speedily as I could. At times, I skipped a few steps by leaping over the railing onto the other side.

"You can't run from me forever!" the creature exclaimed. Its voice echoed and thundered throughout the building. I didn't stop to see how far it had managed to catch up to me. My adrenaline was rushing through me as I just wanted to reach the gym hall as quickly as possible.

"Your death is inevitable!" the creature screeched and I felt panic rushing through me. I frowned as I continued descending to the ground floor.

"Keep your head in the game, Jeanny," I said to myself as I sighed in relief, reaching the last few steps to the ground floor. I skipped the last four steps and landed in the corridor. Grunting and huffing, I ran as fast I could down the corridor. If I had looked behind me, I would've seen the black vein like roots crawling on the walls, ceiling and floor but I was too focused on reaching my destination.

I burst through the double doors. All the spirits that were there looked up at my loud entrance. I barricaded the door like I had done with Brian earlier.

"Positions everyone!" I cried.

*'What if we can't do it?'* Anne asked in the dim moon light that shone from the windows on the ceiling.

I hurried over to her. "Harness energy from me then if you feel like you're too weak to do this. You wanted revenge on this thing, so here's your chance."

Anne's eyes lit up with rage that immediately erased the doubt from her mind, *'I'm going to enjoy this...'* she said in a sadistic tone of voice. I nodded at her with approval, glad that I had sparked her in a way that would benefit not only me but everyone else. I hurried to the back of the line of spirits. The doors to the gym began to bang and rattle loudly. I stared at the door with the dagger in my hand. Silence began to fill the room as tensions rose. Everyone was fixated on the doors waiting for the moment the creature would break through and pounce.

"I'm coming for you, pretty thing!" the creature roared as it ripped and slashed at the door like a knife through paper.

"You have to catch me first!" I bellowed back. I was in truth terrified of this creature, yet I wasn't at the same time. Something was shielding me, it made me remember that I was indeed protected from evil. I quickly shifted my flashlight to my right hand and with my other I placed my fingertips on the necklace I wore. A sudden surge of energy rushed through me as I grasped my flashlight tightly with my left hand and the dagger in my right. The doors began to rapidly shake and shudder that seconds later, they both collapsed onto the floor causing a massive cloud of dust to arise.

"Where are you, little thing?!" the creature said as it stepped over the doors and entered the gym. I decided I didn't want to speak out loud now he was in the same room as me. I watched as the spirits waited until for creature to emerge from the dust cloud.

"Where are you…?" the creature said with a sadistic and alluring tone of voice. As it emerged, I observed how all the spirits dashed off towards him. A whole swarm of entities encircled it. It roared in frustration as it slashed at the spirits with its claws. I was momentarily paralysed with amazement, had it not been for Johnny calling out to me, *'Jeanny! Hurry!'* I would have stayed that way. I shook my head and ran towards the spirits and creature holding the dagger firmly in my hand ready.

"Get off of me, you annoying ants!" the creature roared. I watched as some of the spirits had to withdraw as they had slashes in their spiritual forms.

*Did the creature hurt them even when they were not human?* I asked myself. I continued to charge at the creature suppressing any thoughts and questions in the back of my mind. My dagger made contact with the creature as it roared in agony. I looked up at the creature and saw that the dagger had pierced its heart. It didn't seem at all pleased as it glared at me with death-defying eyes.

"Y... You..." it said growling.

"Go back from whence you came, wretched miscreant!" I roared. I watched as the creature took a few steps back. I expected it would stumble backwards and die. As I turned to the left to look at the spirits, I didn't see his claws slashing down and ripping open my right shoulder. I yelped in pain as I stumbled backwards. The creature laughed at me as it had my blood on its claws. He pulled his hand towards his mouth and licked it all off. I felt disgusted.

"My... my... my..." it began as it struggled to speak. "You... truly are... Simon and Phoebe's daughter. Within yourself there is a lot of potential when it comes to the supernatural and paranormal... Pity though..." It paused to take a deep breath. I, myself couldn't imagine how it would feel to have an object lodged right in my heart.

"You would've... been a special feast... to devour..." the creature said staring at me. I watched as its eyes rolled back and it collapsed backwards onto the ground with a loud thud. I sank to my knees and held onto my right shoulder with my left hand. I lifted my head and stared at the spirits gathered around me.

*'We did it!'* Anne said with excitement. She clapped her hands and giggled. *'That is what you get, you sick bastard!'*

"We barely managed…" I said softly. *I need a break.* I thought to myself. I looked over to the monster that lay there motionless and let out a deep sigh. My right arm was in pain as I whimpered softly. I must've sat on the floor for about five or ten minutes while the spirits conversed with one another.

Johnny approached me. *'Are you alright?'* He asked after a while.

I nodded. "I'll cope." I turned my attention to the spirits around me. "The creature is dead now… It has been vanquished. You may all now go and rest in peace." I watched as the spirits looked at one another.

"T… They are not going anywhere…" I turned my attention to the creature. It crawled back onto its feet and pulled the dagger from its chest. All the spirits that surrounded me backed away.

*'What did Simon tell you to do?!'* Charles, who was one of the few who stood by me, said.

I scrambled to my feet and took a few steps back. "He told me to grab the dagger and stab him!" I said in response with panic in my voice.

*'That idiot!'* Charles said cursing. *'Did he not tell you?!'* I watched as the creature walked towards me grinning sadistically.

"Aw. You set up such a wonderful plan there, Jeanny, but it appears I was granted another chance to devour you after all."

"Told me what?!" I said to Charles taking stepping back more quickly.

*'He forgot to tell you that you needed to rip that amulet from his neck, didn't he?!'* Charles said. I nodded and saw the creature pull out the corresponding amulet from the depths of the black goo on its body.

"Oh, this little thing?" the creature said with a smirk.

*'It makes him immortal, Jeanny! Run!'* Charles said.

"That's right. As long as I have my amulet, I will live on forever! Hahaha!" the creature said sneering.

"Great… Now I have to touch this thing…" I said to myself with discouragement. I gulped and frowned at it. We began to circle one another as if we had just entered the arena of life and death back in the day.

"Prepare yourself, little one," the creature hissed. I repositioned my feet and watched him carefully. I had to use all my knowledge of survival. I closed my eyes and took a deep breath. As I opened my eyes again, the creature lunged at me. I hastily stepped to the creature's right side and grasped his wrist with my right hand, shoving my right knee straight into his gut. The creature gasped in pain. I straightened the creature's arm and slammed my left elbow on his, bending it the other way and breaking it. The creature roared in pain as I continued applying pressure on his broken arm. Due to the sudden assault, it dropped the dagger from its hand and it fell on the floor with a loud thud.

"Let me go!" the creature winced.

"Not a chance!" I said hissing. I continued to apply pressure to his arm as I attempted to reach his collar. Hissing at me loudly, the creature grasped my free arm with its claws. It used its claws to rip my skin open. I gasped in pain and watched helplessly as my blood trickled down to the floor. Angered, I applied enough pressure to its broken arm that it felt I was going to rip it off. The creature cried in so much pain that I forced it onto its knees. I quickly managed to get a hold of the chain of the amulet. I yanked it off from the creature's neck.

"NO!" the creature screeched as it watched me throw the amulet over our heads. It shifted its full attention on the amulet that landed somewhere behind us with a soft metal thud.

"What have you done?!" it screeched. I gritted my teeth in disgust as I swung my left leg at the back of its head. It stumbled forwards onto the ground. It grunted in pain as it tried to get back onto its feet.

"How dare you!" it hissed. I wandered to the dagger that was only a foot away and picked it up. I firmly gripped the handle in my right hand. I stared at the creature with cold and empty eyes. I had legitimately had enough and wanted it all to end.

"You have terrorized these poor souls for way too long…" I began. The creature was obviously fearful of me as the dagger shone brightly in the moon's rays.

"You do not have the heart and guts to kill me." the creature said.

"It's time you return to where you belong," I said calmly.

"Never!" it hissed. It scrambled on its two feet, placed its hands on its chest and glared at me confidently.

"Well, go on," it said with a smirk. I glared at him quietly. There was a long pause between us.

"See? You are weak!" it roared as it dashed towards me. It stretched its arms forward. I held the dagger steadily in my hand. I stepped aside as it passed me. The creature turned around and tried to grab me. I managed to duck out of its reach and leg-swiped him to the floor. It fell towards the ground grunting in pain. I approached it hastily with my right arm raised. I whimpered in pain from my injury but that didn't stop me forcing the dagger straight into the monster's heart while I knelt beside it. The creature cried in pain. Smoke began to emanate from its black goo. Fire emerged quickly from nowhere. I had to crawl away from the fire as the creature was engulfed by flames in a matter of seconds. I scrambled back to my feet as I watched the body turn into nothing but ash. I panted heavily as I shifted my gaze towards the spirits. They were smiling at me. Some of them were waving me farewell as they changed from their human-like manifestations into small white anomalies before disappearing. Anne, Charles and Johnny appeared in front of me.

*'Jeanny... I just want to thank you so much for saving us...'*

I looked at her with a smile. "I'm just glad you can all find some rest..."

*'You saved us all...'* Johnny said.

I shook my head, "It was all of us who managed to accomplish this. Thank you for helping me..." Johnny and Anne smiled at me. I returned the same and nodded. I looked over to Charles who lowered his gaze. I tilted my head a little, "You okay Charles?"

He looked up at me. *'I am sorry about your injuries, Jeanny. They could've been avoided if you only knew...'*

I raised my hand to stop him and shook my head. "You do not have to apologize to me, Charles. What's done, is done. I'm still alive and you are all ready to go to the other side where your ancestors are waiting."

I watched as Charles perked up a little. *'Promise me you'll stay safe and help other spirits when you can...'*

"I promise," I said smiling. "May you all find peace and happiness." They nodded in approval as they transformed into orbs and disappeared into the night. I looked around the gym and saw I was the only one left.

"It's time for me to go home..." I said softly. I wandered towards my dropped flashlight. I kneeled down and packed it away. I quickly checked in my backpack if there was anything that could help with my wounds. I remembered my grandmother handing me a first aid kit. I pulled it out and used the flashlight to illuminate the room to help me find what I was looking for. I decided to use the alcohol-free cleansing wipes to wipe the blood off on my arm and clean the wound. I yelped in pain at the amount of stinging I had to endure. Once I knew it was clean, I decided to use the can of spray plaster. I ensured there was at least two layers on it before wrapping a large sterile gauze dressing over the wounds to keep them clean. The wounds on my back took me longer as I had to be somewhat flexible to clean them. Again, the alcohol didn't make the pain any easier to cope with. I decided to only use spray plaster on my right shoulder.

Satisfied I was all patched up, I put everything away in my backpack and wandered my way to the double doors of the gym. Something shining caught my attention in the corner of my eye. I turned my head and remembered I had tossed the amulet away. I looked back at the spot where the creature burned to ashes. Only the dagger rested there with its tip stuck in the ground. I sighed and decided to take the dagger and the amulet with me. I placed both items safely in my backpack and made my way to the exit.

**<u>Chapter 13</u>**

As I exited the building the same way I entered, a voice caught my attention, calling out my name. I immediately recognized the voice as my little brother Phillip's. I hurried over to where I suspected he was calling from.

"Phillip?!" I called out.

"Jeanny!" I heard him calling out from the school's courtyard. As I arrived, I saw my little brother standing in front of Brian who held a knife against his throat.

I rolled my eyes and gave out a loud sigh. *When is this night ever going to end happily?* I thought to myself.

"You finally decided to come out of this haunted place," Brian said. I nodded and made my hands into fists.

"Let him go, Brian. He's your son for heaven's sake…" I said trying to talk some sense into him.

*'I'm sorry… I wish I was able to warn you sooner, but I couldn't…'* Simon said as he appeared beside me.

"It's fine," I whispered. I frowned and pointed at Brian. "Please release him, Brian!"

"Or else you'll do what?" Brian said pressing the blade against Phillip's skin.

"I don't have to do anything, Brian. Has your obsession with alcohol influence clouded your judgement to the point that you haven't realized there are armed police standing by the gate with drawn tasers and guns?" I said.

"Yeah right. There are no officers there," Brian said arrogantly. I shook my head at his stupidity. I looked at Phillip who was standing there terrified.

"Hey… Phillip?" I said in my kindest tone of voice. "You'll be alright. Just stay strong for me, okay?" Phillip nodded and Brian barked at me to stop talking to his son.

"Sir! Let the boy go and drop your weapon to the floor!" an officer said barking an order directly at Brian. I saw Brian widen his eyes and turn Phillip towards the police as a shield. He pressed the knife closer to the boy's throat. Blood started to trickle from his wound. Phillip began to cry as he was frightened.

"Don't come any closer!" Brian barked. Six other officers pointed their tasers and guns at Brian. James stood behind the police officers with Marion at some distance.

"Brian… It's over for you. Let Phillip go. There's no use in you keeping on denying what you did to my mother and my father," I said calmly. I realized how exhausted I truly was. I was in pain and just longed to be home with my loved ones. I watched as Brian glared at me.

"You do not understand anything! I loved your mother!"

"So did Simon and you killed him!" I snapped.

"He didn't deserve her! She was mine and mine alone!" Brian barked.

"How would you have known that?! You just couldn't stand that someone made her smile with happiness every single day! You were creeping her out with your ridiculous attempts, giving her flowers and wooing her with your pathetic poems!"

"How…" Brian looked at me in shock.

"I understand you loved my mother…" I began, "…but she deserved happiness and you robbed her of that." I could feel Simon's gaze upon me as I spoke. "You went about conquering her heart all wrong… You should've let her decide who she wanted to be with rather than killing someone she cared for and loved. You broke her heart just so you could fulfil your own greed and desires… If you truly loved her, you wouldn't have broken her heart like you did 16 years ago…" A tear slithered down my cheek as I watched Brian stare at me in utter shock and hatred. He pushed Phillip towards the gate and walked up to me with the knife in his hand. I quickly motioned the police to wait. Marion, luckily, picked up the hint and quickly told the officers.

"Hold your fire!" the first officer said. I glared at Brian. I clutched my fists as I watched him raise his hand in an attempt to stab me with the knife. I managed to swiftly dodge the assault. I ducked under his arm and punched him straight in his Adam's apple. Brian glared at me with shock as he gasped for air. He held his throat with his free hand. He dropped the knife and collapsed on one knee. I kicked the knife towards the gate away out of his reach and stared down at him. He returned the gaze with what I could only describe as a pure focus on killing me. I gave the police officers a sign they were free to approach. I walked up to them slowly and they hurried past me. The one officer walked up to me. "Are you alright?"

"Yes," I said nodding. "I'm fine, but you might want to get Brian into an ambulance to check out his Adam's apple. It might suffocate him if not put back into place…"

"Where did you learn this technique, miss?" the officer asked.

"Something called self-defence classes," I responded.

The officer smirked. "You're a clever young girl. Just pray that this guy doesn't die from suffocation, alright?" I nodded. "And make sure you give your witness statement to one of my officers."

"Will do…" I said. I watched as the officer pulled his walkie talkie out and barked some instructions to dispatch. I walked up to Phillip and helped him up. He hugged me tightly. I whimpered a little in pain but I pushed that aside when James and Marion walked up to me.

"You alright, Phillip?" I asked. Phillip looked up at me and cried his little eyes out. I softly wiped them with my thumbs. He nodded at me and hid his face in my stomach once more. I watched as an ambulance pulled up in the distance.

My grandmother Marion came in for an embrace that pulled my attention back to my family. "I'm so glad everyone's okay!" she said with such delight. I chuckled a little and nodded. Something pulled my attention away from my family as I looked over to where Simon was. He wandered away from the courtyard to a more enclosed area.

"Give me a minute, Grandmother…" I said.

My grandmother looked at where Simon stood and then back at me. She smiled. "Go on." I nodded and watched as paramedics escorted Brian to the vehicle on a stretcher.

I hurriedly followed Simon to the edge of the forest where I had learned the truth about him, my mother and the school. I saw him floating next to the boulder with his back turned towards me. As I came closer, he began to speak, *Jeanny… you saved my friends and my school comrades. You have fought and put the murderer to justice.*

"It wasn't much of a big deal…" I started. "A little fight with what I think was a demonic entity that held everyone you knew captive and fed on them like cattle."

*Indeed…* Simon said lowering his gaze. He turned himself to face me as he looked at me sadly.

"Are you trying to tell me something Simon?" I asked. "Are you wanting to tell me you're going to cross over?" He nodded and I bit my lip.

*'Yes… Unfortunately, I do have to cross over. However, before I do, I just want to tell you that I am so proud of you,'* he said with a kind smile.

"Thank you…" I whispered as I returned the smile. "I do want to admit that I'm happy I got such a cool dad."

Simon chuckled a little. *'Me? Cool? Nah!'*

"Oh… I wanted to tell you something Charles said you forgot to mention to me." I said.

*'What is it?'* Simon asked.

"Remember you told me I had to stab that demon in the chest with the dagger?" Simon nodded. "Well, you may have forgotten to fill in the information about the amulet," I added.

Simon sunk his head in defeat. *'How could I have been so dumb? Forgetting something that crucial!'*

"Hey…! It's not such a big deal!" I said trying to comfort him. "I survived and all the others have gone into the light. Don't blame yourself for something this small. I don't want you to be stuck in limbo because you feel guilty about a little thing," I said.

Simon redirected his gaze to me and smiled, *'You'll grow up to be a strong woman someday and remember that me and your mother will always be proud of you.'*

"Thanks, Dad…" I said, whispering, feeling like crying. I watched as Simon turned to look towards the forest.

*'There's your mother…'* Simon said whispering. I followed his gaze and my heart made a small leap of happiness and sadness. She stood there with a white and golden halo waving at me and Simon. I couldn't help but smile with tears slithering down my cheeks. Simon returned the wave to my mother as turned back to me. *'Will you be okay?'*

"I will miss you guys so much…" I whispered. "But I'll be okay knowing that you have found each other…"

Simon chuckled. *'We certainly did find one another and I am proud to call you my daughter.'* He approached me and kissed me gently on my forehead. I expected the contact with my skin to be ice cold; however, surprisingly, it was heart-warming. He backed away and turned to look at my grandmother who had seemingly followed me to make sure I was okay. Simon gave Marion a slight nod and I turned my head to look at her. She must've seen my mother because tears of delight trickled down her face.

'Jeanny?' I looked back to my father. *'I have to go now. Just know that your mother and I love you unconditionally.'*

"As I love you…" I said. I watched as Simon backed away and wandered his way to my mother, Phoebe. She reached out to him with her hand and he grabbed hers in return. They turned to look at me for the last time before they vanished in a halo of light.

### Two Weeks Later

I entered an office. The plaque on the door read C. Tacida. I was dressed formally in a simple beige dotted dress with a cute belt around my waist. I knocked on the door as a man looked up from his computer.

"May I help you?" he asked.

"Are you Mr. Tacida from Dragon House Publishing?" I asked uncertainly to ensure I was speaking with the right person.

"Yes, I am," the man said with a smile. "Are you Jeanny who spoke on the phone with me about your mother's work?"

I nodded. "Yes, that's me."

"Please have a seat," he said standing up and offering me a seat opposite him. I thanked him and sat on the seat.

"How can I help you today?" he asked again.

"I'm here with some of my own and my mother's manuscripts that you wanted me to bring for a proper read through, and perhaps even give them a chance of being published?" I said.

"Yes! Yes!" Mr. Tacida said with excitement and a huge smile. "You are one of the youngest most talented writers we've heard from. Thank you for giving us an insight into your own and your mother's work. Let's discuss your future with us!" I smiled and thanked him.

*"Who knew one would change so drastically after such a life-or-death experience? If you must know… I went back to school, submitted my report about the abandoned school and was given a B+. Besides school, I continued to write just as*

*passionately as my mother, whose works were so successful that they became bestsellers on the market. I was happy that I secured a contract with a publisher as well, so I am on my way to becoming a professional author.*

*Are you wondering what happened to my little brother, Phillip? We decided that he would live with my grandmother. Phillip, despite being traumatized by his father, Brian, went back to school like normal. He did see the occasional therapist but, other than that, he was his old little self. He had me for comfort and support if the nightmares plagued him again.*

*My grandmother on the other hand continued to train and teach me more about my gifts and when to use them. I upheld my promise to Charles that I would continue to use my abilities to help spirits in need.*

*James, however, managed to report his mother and sister to the police. He testified against them, about their abuse of him and how mistreated he felt under their care. His whole family is under investigation and until the court has decided where he is going to stay, he's been permitted to stay with my grandmother.*

*Brian was sentenced to prison for life. He was diagnosed with obsessive love disorder and forced by the court to undergo therapy sessions.*

*As for my parents? If only my mother knew how precious her stories were... Yet, despite all of that, I know she and my father are watching me from wherever they are. Whilst their journey came to an end, my own has just begun."*

*~The End~*

**Author's Note:**

I first created TIOLS (The Imprisonment of Lost Souls) as part of a school project back in Switzerland that counted for the majority percentage of the grade that year. The assignment itself was to create a presentation of the dream job, write a journal of its journey and then execute the final project of that job. My initial dream job, back then, was to become an author despite my disadvantages being a multilingual individual.

The passion for writing was all thanks to Mr. Christopher Paolini publishing his first book "Eragon" that drove my inspiration to become an author.

TIOLS was not the first book I was going to publish; I am still working on my first. Nonetheless, my colouring book, *Dragon Letters Colouring Book,* is already available through Amazon. I hope to finish that first one, and then continue to publish more books in the future.

I want to thank all the people I've met and my friends and family for supporting me through this journey and I will continue to pursue my dream of becoming an author.

*Hélaina Allyza V. Makkink*

If you enjoyed this book by Hélaina Allyza V. Makkink, please check out her "Dragon Letters Colouring Book" and her upcoming "Queen Swan Colouring Book".

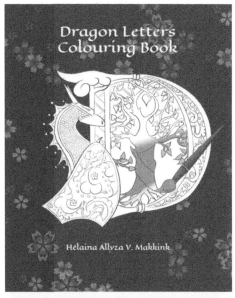

Hélaina Allyza V. Makkink's love of dragons inspired her to read *Eragon* by the author Christopher Paolini and pursue her determination of learning the English language by reading other people's works. She continued to write notes for her Fantasy books and Thriller shorts. She has written filmscripts and directed some short movies along her journey which included *Miseria* and *I Am Anastasia.*

She is now a VTuber on Twitch where she streams a variety of content of games and art providing entertainment to her community whilst being a mother, writer and artist.

Printed in Great Britain
by Amazon

19486867R00161